# RIVERS TRAIL HUNT

A Blue in Kamloops Novel

Alex McGilvery

Rivers Trail Hunt

Alex McGilvery

ISBN: 978-1-989092-83-5



Celticfrog Publishing
Clearwater, BC

# CHAPTER 1
## Tuesday November 16

The drunk staggered into the little coffee shop while Molly was debating the ethics of the latest movie with Tad.

"I'm not saying that the hero gunning all the bad guys down makes a bad ending, but I wish there were consequences." Molly pointed at Tad with the end of her croissant. The tabletop wobbled, but being off in the corner gave them privacy from the few other customers.

"There isn't time at the end of the movie to show an investigation into the hero's action." Tad laughed. "Though I suppose they could do something with the credits."

"You wanna fight?" the drunk leaned against the back of Molly's chair. His breath past her ear made her wince.

"Not particularly." Tad tensed up and Molly put her hand on his.

"Why don't you sit down?" She waved to an empty chair. "It will be easier to talk to you."

"Don't wanna talk, wanna fight." The drunk shook her chair for emphasis, making the table top rock, slopping Molly's coffee.

She mopped it up with the napkin from the croissant. "I'm not the sort to get pulled into a fight." Molly reviewed possible judo moves she could use from her chair. Not many, neither of them were moving so there was no momentum to redirect.

The drunk shook the chair even harder. Molly allowed herself to fall to the floor. She scooted around the table and took a seat across from the drunk. He shoved the chair away and wandered away. Molly sighed with relief, taking deep breaths to calm her heart.

She pulled her coffee over to her and took a slow sip. The drunk came back and picked up what was left of the croissant.

"Wha's this shit?"

"A chocolate croissant." Molly's heart rate spiked again. "Try it, it's good."

"Nah, don't eat shit. He smeared the pastry on the table making the coffee spill.

Tad jumped back to avoid the hot liquid. The drunk leered at Molly.

"Boyfriend's wet his pants." The drunk laughed and tried to tip the table over. When it proved to be fastened to the floor, he swore and grabbed a bottle of sanitizer and sprayed it at her, she blinked to keep it from getting in her eyes. Tad surged out of his chair.

"Don't." Molly held out a hand. The drunk wore filthy jeans and a shirt that might have been stained with blood or ketchup. His knuckles were bloody and swollen. The greasy hair and dirty face gave no clue about the man's age. A ballcap shaded his eyes.

He sprayed Molly again but kept his eyes on Tad. "C'mon I wanna fight, boy."

Tad shook his head and sat down again. "Not interested."

The drunk threw the sanitizer at Tad and snatched a folded knife from his back pocket. Molly went on full attack mode, suppressing the urge to charge in before he got the blade open. Her hands trembled with the effort.

While the drunk fumbled with the knife he lost his grip. The knife clattered on the floor and spun in Molly's direction. She planted her foot on it as the drunk looked around for the knife.

"Where's my knife?" He turned in a circle, then shouted. "Where's my knife?"

"Gone." Molly shrugged.

"I'm gonna kill you." The man clenched his fists and stepped toward Molly.

Tad growled and stood again and dropped into a fighting stance. Molly's gut clenched.

"Maybe it went outside?" Molly said.

The drunk stared at her for a long second, then flipped Tad the bird and left the shop. She watched him searching the sidewalk. Hopefully he'd wander away and forget them. Molly picked up the knife and slipped it into her coat pocket. When she tried to stand up her legs wouldn't cooperate. Tad caught her in hug and held her while she shook.

"There was a day when that wouldn't have bothered me." Molly buried her face in his chest.

"You've been through a lot." Tad squeezed her slightly. "It adds up."

She nodded and wrapped her arms around him.

"Was that man bothering you?" A young man came up to them. "Should I call the police?"

"A little late now." Tad's voice could have been heard through the entire shop, and probably on the street outside.

Molly shook her head and tightened her grip. Tad let out a long breath. "Let's get you home."

She nodded and experimentally stepped back. Her legs didn't collapse. That was a good start. Tad took her hand, the warmth anchoring her in the present. The threat was over.

The young man handed Tad a card. "The manager will be in tomorrow. Call her if you feel you need to."

"I will." Tad's voice still had an edge on it and the young man winced and shrunk into himself.

Molly nodded at him, unable to bring up a smile. Tad led her out the door and scanned the street.

"Looks clear."

"Good."

"You all right to walk to the exchange? I could call a taxi."

"I'll be okay." Molly couldn't stop searching for the drunk.

They walked down Fifth Ave to Lansdowne and over to the exchange. Their bus would be there in twenty minutes.

"I wouldn't have let him hurt you." Tad leaned in the corner of a bus shelter and held her close.

"I wasn't worried about him hurting me." Molly wrapped her arms around herself. "I just didn't want a fight."

"Understandable." Tad said.

The last of the tremors retreated from her body, and Molly relaxed more. The heat of Tad behind her was a welcome buffer against the chill air until the bus came to take them up Fortune to the apartment where she lived with Blue, her friend and adopted father.

At the door to the building, Tad hugged her one last time and kissed the top of her head. He didn't leave until she opened the door to the stairs and gave him one last wave.

***

Blue had gone to bed, so Molly took a long shower to wash away the last of the evening. In her bedroom she climbed under the blankets and lay on her back.

She liked Tad, he was a good friend, but he had to want more from her than friendship. Molly didn't know if she could give it. It wasn't fair. The simple thought of kissing him made her shake even after a year of movie dates. Not that she didn't want to, sort of. She couldn't separate her feelings from the emotions coming from years of trauma.

University had allowed her to put a label on what stood like a brick wall between them.

Molly ran a finger along the scar on her ribs. Anyone who didn't know about it would never see it, but the scar was there, a paler line against her dusky skin. Worse, the memory of what caused it. In a kinder world the girl who tried to kill her might have been a friend. Instead, she'd watched as Carolyn was shot by Sergeant Ferguson to save Molly's life. She still couldn't go to the basement without shuddering.

Blue would suggest she get counselling, she certainly needed it, but how could she bring herself to talk about sex on the street and her desires now? Impossible.

Molly rolled over and pushed the questions and guilt away. Someday she'd face the questions and find answers, but not tonight.

***

## Wednesday November 17

Molly woke trembling from unremembered dreams. She dressed quickly and headed to the kitchen, hoping to catch Blue before he left for work.

He was scrambling eggs and had a cup of coffee brewing.

"How was the movie?"

"The movie was good." Molly put some bread on to toast. "The rest of the evening, not so much."

"What happened?" Blue glanced at her with arched brows.

"Am I being fair to Tad?" Molly shook her head, that wasn't what she wanted to say.

"Has Tad suggested something is missing?" Blue pulled the toast out and put it and the eggs on a plate. Molly put the cup of coffee in front of him as he sat at the table, then sat across from him.

"No, but we've been going to the movies for a year, and I haven't even kissed him good night."

"Has he been wanting to be kissed good night?"

"He stopped asking last March." Molly stared at the table and rubbed at an imaginary crumb. She fought back tears.

"Do you want to kiss him?" Blue said after buttering his toast.

"I don't know." Molly looked up at him. "I'm scared."

"Ah." Blue took a bite of his toast and sipped his coffee. "That does make it hard. I'm not exactly the best person to talk to about kissing."

"Right." Molly sighed. Kelly had drifted out of their lives. It made Molly sad. *I don't want that to happen with Tad.* A tear rolled down her cheek and Blue walked around to put his hand on her back as she dropped her head to the table and gave up fighting the tears.

She finally breathed in and hiccoughed. "You're going to be late for work."

"I'm the boss, I think I can take time to comfort my daughter." He rubbed her back.

"I'll be all right now." Molly stood up and hugged Blue tightly. "Thanks."

"You sure?" Blue patted her back. "I can stay with you if you need."

Molly let go and stepped back rubbing her eyes. "I'm sure." She drew in a ragged breath.

Blue looked at her doubtfully but nodded. He sat back at the table and finished his breakfast in a few bites. "You have the coffee. I'll get one at the Café. Call me if you change your mind."

The door closed behind him, and Molly slumped in a chair at the table, pulled the coffee over and sipped it. She focussed on the rich taste and the heat in her mouth. By the time she'd emptied the cup, all the jagged pieces in her had fallen into enough order for her to organize her messenger bag for the day.

She'd need to grab a couple water bottles and granola bars at work. Walking over to the office on Tranquille would settle the last of the trembling. She made a sandwich and stuffed it into her bag.

The air was chillier than last night, and frost still lay on the ground in the shade. Molly pulled her collar up. *Should have eaten breakfast.* She veered over to McDonalds and ordered breakfast burritos.

Someone waved her over and Molly recognized a woman she'd help find housing. The rental market was still so tight that some people lived in their cars while they went to work.

"Good morning, Vickie." Molly sat at the table and unwrapped the first burrito. "How's the new place?"

"The girls are mad they don't have their own rooms and we had to get rid of a lot of furniture and stuff, but they're happy in the new school and have already made some friends. The boys next door play their music too loud and the people upstairs sound like they're dribbling basketballs. It's heaven compared to living in the car." Vickie laughed. "I can't thank you enough for the help you gave us. We want to give back a little. Is there any way we can help your work?"

"Thank you." Molly took another bite and gave it some thought. "There is a campaign going on now collecting gloves, socks, and toques for people on the street. Look for Kamloops Helps on facebook."

"I'll do that." Vickie smiled and finished her sandwich. "Thanks again. I need to get to work." She stood up and nodded to Molly before leaving the restaurant.

Molly finished her breakfast and walked the rest of the way to the office.

Molly pushed the intercom button. "I bumped into a client on the way here and chatted for a bit." Sally made a note and buzzed Molly through the door to the back.

Molly stopped at the cupboard for water and granola bars, then headed for her manager's office.

"Good morning." Don said and waved to the chair. "You were late again, missed the briefing."

"Sorry, I checked in with someone on the way here."

Don sighed. "I get that you want to talk to your clients but getting here on time is also important. You can always schedule a time to meet with them later."

"Okay Don." Molly said repressing the feeling she was a child being lectured to by disappointed teacher. "Sorry, I will do that in the future."

"Very well." Don leaned back. "You will work out of the office today since you weren't at the briefing. Nothing much out of the ordinary."

"Thank you, Don." Molly waited for him to wave her out of his office and until she was out in the hallway to sigh. She didn't like working the office. There was little to do between clients and then she'd get a bunch of them at the same time and be frantic that people would leave before she got to them.

The phone buzzed and she picked it up.

"Someone out front for you." Sally said and hung up. Molly stood and checked herself. She didn't want to carry extraneous emotions into the meeting. She picked up a clipboard with the intake form and a pen.

As the door to the offices closed behind her, Molly looked around for the client. He was the drunk from last night, still wearing the stained and filthy clothes. He stared at her but gave no indication that he knew who she was.

"I'm hungry."

"The Loop just down Tranquille will be open now."

"Can't go there. Got in a fight last week." The man flexed his hands, still bloody and swollen. "No one likes me."

"Have you thought about why you keep getting into fights?" Molly stayed where she was a safe distance from the man.

"Everyone's an asshole," the man muttered. "I'm hungry."

"Answer a few questions and I'll get you a couple of granola bars."

"Fine." He slouched in the chair and picked at the scabs on his knuckles.

"What's your name?"

"Dennis Colm."

"How long are you banned from The Loop?"

"Rest of the week."

"Are you banned from anywhere else?"

"Everywhere." Dennis stared at his shoes.

"What services have you accessed recently?"

"No one will talk to me." He glared at Molly.

"Interior Health runs groups that may help you fit in better."

"Don't want no groups, full of assholes."

"Aside from food, what is your most immediate need?"

Dennis lifted his head and met Molly's gaze.

"To be left alone. Everyone wants me to do this or do that, fuck'm. Are you giving me food or not?"

Molly knocked on the glass and the door buzzed open. "I'll be right back."

She raided the cupboard for a couple bars and a bottle of water before returning to the front. "Here you are Dennis."

He curled his lip at the bars but took them and stuffed them into his pocket. "Don't drink water." Dennis stomped out the door, and Molly sighed before asking Sally to buzz her in again. She didn't have time to write up the encounter before the phone buzzed and Sally announced another client. Putting another intake form on the clipboard, Molly headed for the front.

It was going to be a long day.

# CHAPTER 2
## Wednesday November 17

Blue looked up from his paperwork when Tad knocked on the door frame.

"Come in." He pushed the pile aside and waved toward the chair.

"Sorry to bother you, but I'm worried about Molly." Tad frowned.

"How so?"

"Did she tell you what happened last night?"

"We got onto a different topic." Blue leaned back. "Tell me about it."

"We were getting coffee after the movie like always when this drunk came in and tried to pick a fight." Tad went on to describe the incident and Molly's reaction.

"I see." Blue put his elbows on the desk. "Are you all right?"

"Yeah, sure." Tad frowned. "It wasn't that big a deal for me. I was more worried about Molly getting hurt or something."

"Right." Blue remembered a time when he was like that; sure he could handle every situation. Then he couldn't and it sent him on a downward spiral he took years to pull out of. "Maybe worry about yourself a little. Molly wouldn't like it if you got hurt."

"Okay." Tad stood up. "I just wanted to let you know." He left the office.

Blue sighed. He hoped Tad wasn't too upset at the suggestion he could get hurt. The paperwork wasn't going to do itself and he needed to get it done before he went out to the front of the Café.

He finished up before lunch and stepped into the Café to eat with the guests. He knew most of them by name. A pair of old men sat at a corner table playing cards. They shared a tiny apartment but were lonely being there all day just the two of them. Sometimes Blue joined their game for a while, but Jack and George were mostly content to sit in the bustle of the Café.

Myrtle had her electric wheelchair pulled up to another table an extension cord snaking from the chair's battery to the wall plug. Getting her that chair was one of the Café's major victories.

Erica had Agatha parked at a table. The older woman still struggled with the fallout of a brain injury the year before, but Erica was good for her. Agatha was good for Erica too, she was less likely to work extra-long hours in the Café. Having someone at home to care for helped her relax.

"Hey, Blue take a load off." Agatha waved him over.

He sat across from her. "Morning Agatha."

"How's Molly doing?" Agatha grinned.

"Keeping busy as an outreach worker for Streetreach up the road."

"She's going places, that girl." Agatha's smile widened. They had this conversation on a regular basis, but Agatha's smile never failed to warm him.

"She is that." Blue accepted a bowl of soup and a slice of bread from Erica, who put a meal in front of Agatha before heading over to serve other people.

"Too bad we didn't win the election last year, but some interesting stuff is happening." Agatha dipped her bread in the soup.

"You had an impact even if you didn't win."

Agatha waggled a finger. "My name may have been on the ballot, but Molly did all the important work."

Blue spooned up his soup, cream of cauliflower today, the bread was a dark rye. He ate his lunch and listened to Agatha's words flow.

***

Molly sat at her desk eating her sandwich. The paperwork on her desk called to her, but Don told them again and again that they needed to care for themselves to be able to help others. She turned away from the desk and looked out the barred window to the alley. There would be workers talking to the people, listening to the chatter.

She wanted to do social work, not paperwork, yet the endless reports and forms she filled out were a vital part of any grant application. *Can't have one without the other.* Stuffing the last of the sandwich into her mouth and washing it down with tepid coffee from the staff room, Molly turned back to the desk.

Just as her shift was ending, Sally phoned from the front.

"We've got a live one."

Molly picked up the clipboard, made sure a fresh form was at the ready, and headed to the front. She'd seen the man before on her shifts outside. He wore a long trench coat of an undetermined grey. A fedora of the same colour sat on his head. Blue eyes peered out from beneath the brim.

"I need to talk to you." He looked around quickly, frowning at Sally. "Alone."

Molly opened the door into a small interview room. She waved the man into sit on the other side of the room, away from the door.

"They won't hear?" the man asked, squinting at her suspiciously.

"The room is soundproof. No one can listen in unless I push that button." She pointed to the panic button beside the door then sat down in the chair facing the client.

The man perched on the chair as if ready to bolt, but relaxed slightly. "We'll have to risk it."

"What's your name?" Molly poised her pen over the form but took several breaths before the man whispered to her.

"Edwin Smith." He scanned the room again.

"What kind of help are you looking for?"

"I've run out of rations." Ed looked at his feet. "I can't buy anything without them knowing."

"There are few places who provide meals at no cost."

"No names?" His hand clamped on his knees.

"No names." Molly stood and picked up a pamphlet from the display on the wall. "Here's list of places along with the days and times. There's a map on the back to show you where they are."

Edwin held the map close to his face. "Clever." He folded the pamphlet and put it in an inner pocket and stood up.

"Other than food what is your most immediate need?" Molly asked.

"Have to stay out of sight, or they'll get me." Edwin pulled his hat down over his eyes and slipped out the door.

Molly sighed and looked at the form. She had his name and nothing else.

"Don't feel bad," Sally handed her a file. "He's not a regular, but he's been here before."

"Thanks," Molly carried the paper back to the office. Sally opened the filing cabinet and showed Molly a folder. It was filled with forms and reports, all with a different name, but one thing in common. The grey trench coat and fedora. The label on the file read 'Trench coat guy.'

He mostly asked for food, but there was a referral to a public health nurse and another to Interior Health for an assessment. Molly added her notes to the file and set it aside to give back to Sally. The other files and reports were complete. They too would go to Sally for filing. Some of the clients coming through the door knew their file numbers. Others Sally recognized and pulled the file. Molly made a last check to make sure she hadn't missed anything.

Time to head home and think about what to cook for supper. She didn't feel like eating a frozen meal, though they took a weekend a month to prepare them.

"I'm off Sally," Molly said on her way out. Sally was dressed for the cold, but she took the number 2 bus to the exchange on Lansdowne, then up the hill to her home in Sahali. Sally waved as Molly stepped out the door. Sally would lock it and the back door before leaving.

It was on the walks home through the cold or wet when Molly dreamed about having a car. Where she'd park it or pay for it, who knew? The daydream took her all the way to the apartment. She let herself into the building and climbed the stairs.

Blue wasn't home yet, probably had a meeting of some kind. Molly texted to let him know she was home.

She chopped veggies and put rice on for a stir fry. Some frozen meat would add substance to the meal. They always had various cubed meat for quick cooking. Molly hummed as she cooked, for the immediate moment, trauma and worries banished from her being.

Blue came in the door and breathed in deeply. "Smells great."

"Almost ready. You have just enough time to wash up." Molly set the table. Her phone rang.

"Hi." Molly put the phone on speaker and checked the rice, it fluffed up nicely.

"Molly," Ciara said. "There's a movie I want to see, but Grandma won't let me go alone. Going with Dean doesn't count. I'm begging you to come with me."

Molly laughed. "When is this movie? And what's the movie?" Her niece was a handful. She walked a fine line between being a normal teen girl and a rebellious hellion.

"It's Friday night." Ciara's voice squeaked with excitement. "It's some dramatic thing, but I know someone who's in the movie and I promised I'd go see it."

"Okay, I can make it work."

Ciara's squeal of excitement made Molly wince.

"Thank you, thank you, thank you. I'll tell grandma."

"Give her a hug for me." Molly hung up.

"Ciara?" Blue walked into the kitchen.

"We're going to a movie on Friday, details to follow."

"Busses aren't regular that time of night."

"I'm thinking we can bus it to the Paramount. And ask Hanna to pick us up after the show. I'll stay there for the night. It will give me a chance to catch up with Hanna and Ciara."

"Sounds good, I will look forward to the full report Saturday evening."

"A redacted report, there will be girl talk."

Blue held his hands up and laughed. "Okay, okay. I don't need to hear about the girl talk." He sat down and Molly put the rice and stir fry on the table.

"Dig in." She took a chair across from him and served herself after Blue took his. There would leftovers for the next day.

"Tad stopped by my office." Blue pushed away from table a bit.

"Oh?"

"He told me about what happened at the coffee shop."

"Oh." Molly's mood dropped. "I was going to tell you this morning, but my mouth took off without me."

"No problem." Blue smiled at her. "I know you tell me things when you're ready to."

"It wasn't so much the guy." Molly knotted her fingers together. "I was scared Tad would step in and get hurt."

"That's why you shook all the way home?" Blue tilted his head.

"I had a trauma reaction after the guy left." Molly held her hands still, but the trembling in her chest made her want to curl up beside Blue and sleep.

"Did that connect with this morning's conversation?"

Molly gasped and concentrated on breathing until she could speak.

"Tad was so good. He backed off when I asked him, then made sure I got home in one piece. Some party of me wonders why."

"He cares about you."

"Why would he?" Molly said. "He goes to all that trouble, and I give him nothing in return."

"Has he asked for anything?" Blue held up a hand. "Friendships aren't about keeping a balance sheet."

"I know that." Molly rubbed her temples, "but a part of me is always waiting for the demand for something I can't give him."

"That would be a problem." Blue said. "Remember, it took a while for you to trust me. But it worked itself out. Maybe the challenge is to learn to trust Tad to be just himself. Be friends and enjoy each other's company."

"You're right." Molly's gut burned, but she didn't know why she should be angry at Blue. Not Tad either. "Thanks." She fled to her room and lay on her bed fighting to unclench her fists.

Blue would be worried about her, but he wouldn't say anything. He was always good at giving her space to work things out. Molly rolled to her feet and changed for bed, suddenly exhausted. She fell into her bed, hugged her pillow, and finally fell asleep.

# CHAPTER 3
## Friday November 19

Ciara bounced with excitement. Her favourite aunt was taking her out to a movie. A movie in which she knew one of the actors. She wondered for a moment if she wanted Dean along, but Molly hadn't met him, and things could get weird.

"Calm down," Grandma waved her wooden spoon at Ciara. Molly will be here soon enough."

"It's been ages since Molly had supper with us, and she's staying the night!" Ciara pirouetted and Grandma laughed.

There was a knock and Molly stuck her head in the door.

"Hello."

Ciara bolted over and hugged Molly, wet snowy coat, and all.

"The weather looks nasty out there." Grandma waited for Molly to hang up her coat before hugging her and showing her into the kitchen. "I think I will drive you to the theatre as well as picking you up. It will give us more time at supper."

Molly smiled and nodded. "I wasn't looking forward to walking in the snow. I only have my light coat; I need a new heavy coat. I'm thinking of hitting the thrift shops this week."

"I'll come with you and help you choose." Ciara clapped her hands.

"Goodness, I'll have to invite Molly over more often if she brings out the cheerful girl in you. Whatever happened to the gloomy teen?"

"Locked her in the closet for the night." Ciara stuck her tongue out at Grandma, and they all laughed. *Why couldn't life be like this all the time? Laughing and joking and carrying on?*

"May have to do some closet cleaning." Grandma said.

"Don't go in my closet." The words burst out of Ciara, spoiling the mood.

"Sorry." Grandma said. "I know you treasure your privacy, and I trust you when you say there is nothing bad in there."

Ciara hugged her grandma and pushed away the grumpy mood. They sat at the table and Grandma served up the moose stew. Ciara rolled her eyes, moose again, but it was a treat for Molly.

"I made the bannock." She pointed to the basket.

"Looks great." Molly sat and picked a piece of bannock to put beside her stew.

Grandma sat down and they dug into the meal.

"What do you do at your job?" Ciara asked between bites.

"Talk to people and do paperwork," Molly groaned. "The paperwork is more boring than schoolwork, it's the same questions every time."

"Why don't you get a better job?" Ciara dipped bannock in the stew.

"To get the job I want, I need to work at jobs I don't like that much. It gives me experience that will help later."

"Like Grandma tells me I need to put up with school before I can do what I want." Ciara tilted her hand back and forth. "I'm not sure about that, but I don't have much choice."

"You have choice about the most important thing." Molly smiled

"Which boy to go out with?" Ciara arched her brows and Molly laughed.

"No, what attitude you bring to school with you. Do you work hard or goof off and cause trouble?"

"Working hard isn't much fun."

"Not until you see the benefits. Like you wanted to learn piano, now look how good you're getting in just a year."

"Math is nothing like piano." Ciara pouted, but then kicked herself. No gloomy teen tonight.

"No that's true, but learning can be fun for its own sake. Challenge yourself and plan a reward for when you succeed." Grandma had that 'I know something you don't' smile on her face. Any other night Ciara would challenge her, and they'd argue. Tonight, she wouldn't do that.

"I will have to think about a suitable reward." Ciara grinned. "That could be expensive."

"Since you are giving the reward to yourself, you can spend as much of your money as you want." Grandma smiled back.

Ciara rolled her eyes, but she added up how much money she could get before the end of school. She had her babysitter certificate, but all the kids she'd watched were brats. Something tickled her mind and she vowed to chase that thought down. Later.

Supper finished with apple pie, and Ciara rated this as one of the best days of her recent life. And she hadn't even gone to the movie yet.

***

The movie was a double bill. Ciara grinned, she never got to stay up this late. They got popcorn and drinks and found seat on the aisle. The lights dimmed and the ad told the people to turn off their cellphones. If she had one, she would have anyway. Nothing would interrupt this perfect night with Molly

Molly turned her phone off. "Good thing I don't have to be on call."

"No kidding." Ciara stuffed popcorn in her mouth.

The first movie was about a girl going to school. It was a nicer school than hers, and all the students drove their own cars. She couldn't decide between two boys, one was a bad boy and the other studious and boring. At first Ciara rooted for the bad boy, she like how he defied authority and did his own thing. But a strange thing happened, she got bored of him. Every time he showed up on the screen, she knew exactly what he was going to do, and a lot of the time it hurt people around him, even the girl he said he loved.

The studious one helped people out. He obviously had it bad for the girl, but he didn't get mad when she went out with the other boy. He tutored the girl in math, so she'd pass her exams and get into university. Ciara wanted the girl to wake up. The guy was boring, at least he didn't get them arrested.

At the big confrontation between the bad one and the boring one. The bad boy talked about how the boring one was a sheep who only cared what other people thought of him. The boring one laughed.

"I don't care what anyone thinks of me. I don't need attention from other people. I live who I want to be as a person."

The bad boy beat up the boring one, but he didn't win the girl. Neither did the boring one. She kept going to him for tutoring and help with things, but decided to go out with a football player.

"I know you're a good person, but I need excitement in my life"

Ciara wanted to strangle her. Sure, the guy looked boring, but he helped so many people, even if they didn't know it was him. Maybe the girl just didn't see that.

She was still complaining to Molly about it as they got popcorn for the next movie.

"What a moron, she needs to open her eyes."

"Maybe she's not ready." Molly said. "Lots of people live for thrills and excitement. It is like an addiction, until she sees who she is, how can she see who other people are?"

"She's still a moron." Ciara said with a definite nod of her head. "I'm facebook friends with a girl from Manitoba. She made a video with Nwe Jinan. I commented how I liked her singing and we got to talking about music and found we like the same stuff. She posted that she'd been in a movie. I was so excited it came here. I can't wait to tell her I saw the movie. She's playing young Claire she said."

The lights went down again, and the movie started.

An old grandmother was trying to help her family, they were all in some kind of trouble, drinking, getting arrested and more. Then a group came to the reserve and asked the elders to tell them stories of their time in residential school. The grandmother's family was shocked and horrified when she stood to tell her story.

That is when the movie shifted to young Claire who was taken away to school along with her brother and sister. The people at the school made her strip and take a shower with strong soap, then cut off her hair. It only got worse from there. Claire didn't care what they did to her, but she tried to keep her brother and sister safe.

Ciara gasped for breath. She'd heard stories about the schools, some from elders on her own reserve. The red brick school towering over the powwow grounds, still demanded attention. But seeing her friend playing this brave girl and being punished again and again for it broke her heart. Molly held her hand as she cried when the younger sister died from illness and just vanished, like she'd never existed. Claire and her brother survived, but he became hard and bitter and stopped talking to Claire who wanted him to find hope in his life. He killed himself and Claire found him and blamed herself for not stopping him. She set herself to live in spite of the school, learned healing, got married, had children and grandchildren trying to teach them to embrace life.

It ended with a close up of old Claire crying while her sons led her back to her seat while everyone stood in complete silence.

Molly sat with her as the credits rolled and pointed out the name of the girl who played young Claire, Ciara couldn't see the screen through her tears. They weren't the only ones in the theatre sitting still and silent.

Finally, Ciara took a deep breath and stopped crying. Molly hugged her and they headed for the exit doors. As they stepped outside Ciara saw a man shouting and waving something around people were running away from him. She held Molly's hand tighter as police cars arrived, sirens blaring to silence and lighting the street in red and blue.

"Come on, let's find your Grandma, the police will deal with it." Molly tugged her along.

Three bangs made Ciara jump and clutch at Molly. She couldn't help but look back. The shouting man had stopped, a body lay still in the flashing lights.

Ciara huddled against Molly who rubbed her back and talked softly about things Ciara couldn't hear. Molly dug out her cellphone and called Grandma to let her know what happened and to where to find them.

Ciara sat in silence all the way home while Molly and Grandma talked softly in the front seat. She wanted to sleep but was afraid to. What if she dreamed about the man?

Grandma and Molly walked her into the house and helped her change into her pajamas like she was a little kid. Ciara didn't care, not if being a little kid would keep her safe.

Molly put to her to bed and covered her up, then lay down beside her on the narrow bed to rub Ciara's back. Every time Ciara shuddered awake, Molly was there to rub her back and wipe away tears.

When the morning light woke her, Ciara squirmed out of Molly's arms and went to take a shower. She still trembled a bit, but the water made her feel better. She went back to her room and got dressed without caring what she wore, then sat in her chair and watched Molly sleep.

Molly looked peaceful, but Ciara knew where to look for the scars. Molly had always been her cool auntie, the one who understood her best. She'd heard some of the stories, obviously edited for her young ears and heart, but now somehow, they were more than stories, they were things that had happened to Molly, things she carried with her like Grandma Claire's memories. Ciara didn't know how Molly could do that, but she wanted to.

Ciara picked up the pad of paper on her desk and started scribbling lyrics, pouring her feelings into words.

# CHAPTER 4
**Friday November 19**

Sergeant Ferguson stood up his collar in a futile attempt to stop the wind and snow going down the back of his neck. Sergeant Hassim had the right idea with a scarf and toque. She argued that they were plainclothes, so they should be comfortable.

It was a distraction from the job at hand. The scene of the police involved shooting was locked down tight as the Scene of Crime people did their job. The Independent Investigations Office would be showing up and would want all the evidence undisturbed. One of the officers setting the perimeter had come across the body in the alley not far from the shooting.

Ferguson got the call. He'd have to dance a bit to keep the IIO scene clean, but hoped the investigators would share anything related to the homicide. For now, he got what he could while waiting for his turn with SoC. He suspected the weapon would prove to be the knife lying beside the body of the man the police shot on the corner.

"Sharp dresser." Hassim crouched to get a different angle on the scene. "That's not a cheap coat. Strange that the only blood comes from a single stab wound to the chest. You'd expect a flurry of wounds from someone as deranged as the man on the ground over there." She waved a hand in the direction of the flashing lights that lit up the end of the alley.

"No assumptions." Ferguson said reflexively, "but it does look like a single blow to the heart. Either the perp knew what they were doing, or they were lucky. The victim must have died almost instantly, there are no stains on his gloves that I can see."

He took pictures with his cell phone. "Want to get some shots before the snow covers any more evidence. No scramble of footprints or sign of struggle in the snow. The prints coming and going are staggering, perhaps belonging to the body out front. No indication of which direction the victim came from, so maybe he was waiting long enough for the snow to cover his prints."

"I'll check with the weather office and see if we can get any idea of snowfall rates from this evening."

"Good idea." Ferguson took more pictures from every angle he could without disturbing the existing prints, but the still falling snow looked to erase them before SoC got on the scene.

"We've finished photographing the first scene." A man in a white tyvex suit came around the corner.

"Awesome. See if you can get any detail from the footprints before we lose them, then whatever else you need."

"Sure." The Scene of Crime person took out a camera and shot a picture of a notebook, then took pictures of the scene from a distance. "Hold your flashlight low to the ground to light up the footprints, we may get enough contrast to pull detail from the shots." He took photos of the corpse as a whole and in detail.

The community coroner showed up and inspected the scene, then took a closer look at the body. She made notes as she went.

"Okay, the people will be here to pick up the body as soon as they can. A team is waiting on scene up there." She nodded her head toward the corner. "Someone else has been called for this one."

"Thank you." Ferguson said.

The coroner waited for transportation to arrive, then supervised the removal of the body.

With the corpse gone, the SoC photographer took another series of photos of where the body had been slumped against the wall.

"You'd think there would be more blood." Hassim said. "There's hardly any on the ground."

"You're right, but the pathologist will have something to say on that." Ferguson walked farther down the alley, shining his light back and forth to search for anything out of place.

"Hey, Hassim, I've got something here."

She joined him and stared at the cart covered with a ragged blue tarp. "Maybe someone was sleeping here. The snow's covered everything, no prints."

"I'll get SoC to tag everything. It may have no connection to the case, but we want to be sure." Ferguson pulled out his phone and reported the new scene. "I'll wait here for SoC, you walk the rest of the alley and check for any other surprises.

"Sure thing." Hassim walked down the alley, but returned before the SoC people arrived. "A whole lot of nothing. Not even much garbage."

They left SoC to tag everything in the cart and went back to the Battle St. station. Ferguson got an occurrence number and opened a file on the case. He uploaded his cell phone pictures and made a brief report of their actions upon arriving at the scene. If it was connected to the officer involved shooting, life was going to get complicated.

***

## Saturday November 20

Ferguson sat at his desk, cup of coffee still steaming, and checked on the case. The victim in the alley was one Pathi Bajwa, a businessman. His home was up in Aberdeen. They would start by interviewing the family. He texted Hassim to meet him at the car, then headed there himself. He poured a lot more coffee than he drank.

Hassim put the address into the maps application and Ferguson negotiated the slick streets up Columbia to Pacific Ave, then through a maze of neighbourhood streets to pull up in front of a substantial home. Two cars sat in the driveway in front of a three-car garage, from the snow on them, they had been there all night. No tracks led to the third garage.

Ferguson knocked on the front door and pulled out his ID, Hassim copied him.

The door opened to a middled age woman in flowing pants and blouse.

"They told me you would be coming." She glanced at the IDs then stepped back. "Please come in."

Ferguson stepped through the door and wiped his shoes on the mat. "You live here by yourself?"

"No, we have three children, they are over at the eldest son's house. You probably already know I am Rutvi Bajwa. We immigrated to this community shortly after we married twenty-six years ago."

"Looks like you've been very successful." Hassim said.

"We were already wealthy when we came. It is easy for the rich to succeed, but my husband took his business seriously and did very well by any measure." Rutvi led them to an immaculate living room and waved a hand at the seats.

"Your husband, you mean Pathi Bajwa?" Ferguson sat in a chair and pulled out his notebook.

"Of course." Rutvi seated herself across from Hassim on the couch. "You were expecting a distraught widow. Pathi and I knew we going to wed since we were children. We weren't 'in love' as your media portrays, but we were good friends and partners. I am sad he died, but I need to be calm so our children can mourn as they need."

"I see." Ferguson made a note.

"If they need someone to talk to, Victim Services is available to help." Hassim passed a card to Rutvi.

"I will let them know." Rutvi took the card and examined it. "They are of an age to make their own decisions about such things."

"Tell me a little about your children?" Ferguson asked.

Rutvi warmed up as she talked about her children. "Peter is the oldest, he just got married to a lovely woman last year. He shares ownership of a car dealership with his father. Pathi didn't want the children to grow up without learning how to work. Pearl is in the arts class at Thompson Rivers university. That painting is one of hers." Rutvi pointed to a large painting hanging over the mantle. It was done mostly in shades of orange, but other colours peeked out. He almost thought he saw a picture under the abstract brush strokes.

"She is very talented." Hassim tilted her head. "I've seen paintings not nearly as striking in galleries in Vancouver."

"Pearl has sold a few paintings, but she is waiting until she graduates before holding a show."

Rutvi smiled warmly and gazed at the painting for a few breaths, then sighed and turned her attention back to Ferguson. "Vikrant is the youngest, he is in grade twelve in high school."

"Sounds like you worry about him the most." Hassim said. "It's hard to be the third child in such a talented family."

"Two of your children have western names, but Vikrant sounds East Indian." Ferguson looked up from his notebook.

"We gave all the children both western and eastern names. When they started school, each decided what they wanted to be called."

"I see." Ferguson made notes in his book. "Tell us a bit about Pathi."

"He was a very diligent man, and an honest one. Pathi liked his comforts, but he never over-indulged himself. Just now he was working on development project with some partners. I can give you their names before you go. He has three sports cars but drives an SUV in the winter because his family's safety is more important than his love of cars."

"Was there anyone who would want to hurt him?" Hassim asked.

"There are people he angered, but I can't see any of them killing Pathi."

"Any recent changes in behaviour?" Ferguson poised his pen over his notebook.

"Pathi didn't tend to routines and such. He would do what was necessary when it was needed. But no, I haven't noticed any changes in his demeanour."

"Did he often have meetings late at night?" Hassim leaned forward slightly.

"No, but sometimes he would have to accommodate someone."

"Do you know what he would have been meeting about last night?"

"He didn't tell me anything." Rutvi frowned.

"Is that unusual?" Ferguson followed up on the change in expression.

"Somewhat." Rutvi's frown deepened. "We were partners in business as in life. But if something came up suddenly, he might have not had time to call."

"So he didn't call last night?"

"No, given the weather I was concerned for his safety." Rutvi blinked rapidly and took a long breath. "I believe I have given you as much time as I am able today."

"We are very sorry for your loss." Hassim stood and put her notebook away. "If you think of anything you want us to know, call us." She handed Rutvi a card. The woman showed them out without saying anything else.

"What do you think?" Ferguson asked as they put their seatbelts on.

"She seemed straight forward enough. I didn't get the impression she was holding back, but she didn't volunteer anything. Everything she said was an answer to a question."

"Except for the bit about their marriage. I had the feeling it was something she feels necessary to explain often. I wonder if Pathi felt the same way." Ferguson tapped his fingers on the steering wheel. "Maybe we'll get something more from the children."

"I forgot to ask for the son's address." Hassim slapped her forehead.

"Don't worry about it. I expect there aren't many Bajwas in Kamloops." Ferguson typed on his phone. "Only two, and one is this address. He put the other address in maps and showed Hassim. "It isn't far from here."

"From what Rutvi said they are all adults." Hassim leaned back. "Let's pay them a quick visit."

A few minutes later they pulled up in front of a smaller house. Ferguson led the way to the front door and knocked.

The door opened and a young man glared at them. "This isn't a good time." He started to close the door, but stopped when Ferguson waved his ID.

"We are very sorry for your loss, but it would be helpful to talk to you now. Only a few minutes."

"Fine then." The young man stepped back and allowed them into the house.

The sound of weeping and hushed conversation greeted them.

"I'm Sergeant Ferguson, and this is Sergeant Hassim."

The young man nodded and led them to a smaller living room, but this one looked like people lived in it, or perhaps the disarray was due to grief.

"Guys, the cops are here to ask questions. They promised to keep it short." The young man slumped in a chair near where an older version of him comforted a woman who looked like a young Rutvi.

"Sorry for your loss." Ferguson said again and took out his notebook. "If I could begin with your names." He wrote them in his notebook as if Rutvi hadn't said anything about the children.

"Anything unusual about your father in the past few days?" Ferguson scanned their faces. They shook their heads. "Anyone you can think of who would want to harm your father?"

Again, they shook their heads.

"What kind of person was your father?"

"I'm taking mechanics when I graduate. Father wanted to make me a partner in his car dealership. I told him I wanted to get my hands greasy, not sit at a desk." Vikrant said. "I don't think he understood."

"Father was like that," Pearl said. "He was always looking for ways to help us out, though he insisted we had to have plans to earn our own money. Unfortunately, he didn't always agree with our plans."

Peter nodded his agreement. "I'm a partner in the dealership, but I'm expected to work and learn how the business is run."

"What other businesses did your father own aside from the dealership?" Ferguson asked.

"Who knows?" Peter wiped his eyes. "He had his fingers in a lot of things, but he wanted us to focus on our own lives, not what he was doing."

"Thank you for your time. If you think of anything else that might help us, give us a call." Ferguson handed each of them cars, one of his and one for victim services.

Vikrant showed them to the door and shut it firmly behind them.

"They seemed genuine." Hassim said. "I'll run backgrounds on them and see if something jumps out at me."

"Good." Ferguson put the car in gear and hoped he remembered how to get out of the maze.

# CHAPTER 5
## Saturday November 20

"Are you sure you want to go shopping?" Molly looked for signs of last night's trauma in Ciara, but only found an eager girl.

"Shopping is the best thing to help me forget stuff for a while." Ciara's smiled dimmed for a moment. "I know forgetting isn't the best thing, but it will help me get through the weekend."

"Shopping it is then." Molly clapped her hands. "Should we start at Value Village?"

"You really don't like buying new things, do you?" Ciara poked Molly. "We can start at Value Village if you promise to buy one new thing for yourself."

"But I don't need anything, really." Molly put her hands up.

"One new thing." Ciara held up a finger. "Or we go straight to Aberdeen Mall."

"Okay, okay." Molly laughed. "I'm looking for a heavy winter coat and maybe some nice winter boots. What are you looking for?"

"Don't know, but I will when I see it." Ciara tapped her purse. "Let's go meet the bus."

They got off the bus at Sahali mall and walked up to the Value Village.

"We'll start with the winter coats." Molly led the way to the racks of winter coats. "Not a lot of selection left."

"How about this?" Ciara held up a leather coat with a fur collar.

"Don't think so." Molly hung it back up. "A little too tight." She rapidly turned down a hot pink ski jacket and a bright orange coat. "I like the colour, but it will look like I've escaped from a road crew. I need something that will keep me warm and look professional."

"Hmm." Ciara put a finger to her temple. "We'll have to get creative. There's nothing on this rack, let's try over there."

"Those are dress coats." Molly said, then picked one off the rack. It looked like a puffy coat and a trench coat combined in a deep burgundy colour.

"Try it on." Ciara put a hand out to hold Molly's light weight jacket.

"Okay." Molly put it on. It fit well over the sweater she was wearing and came down not quite to her knees.

"Looks good, and it will keep you warm while waiting for the bus." Ciara walked around her. "Has good pockets too."

"You think it will be warm enough?" Molly stroked the coat. "It feels awfully light. She took it off and regretfully hung it up.

"Not so fast." Ciara checked the label in the coat. "Never heard of it before, but it says it is made with eider down. Should be warm enough. The price is good too."

"You think so?" Molly tried it on again. "It is nicer than the heavy parka I was thinking about."

"So that's decided, we need to accessorize it." Ciara dragged her over to a wall filled with hats and they tried on after another before settling on a black toque that looked like it was made of fur. Ciara found a scarf to match and stood back sizing up Molly.

"You look gre—"

Something fell with a bang on the other side of the store and Ciara went pale and looked ready to bolt.

"I'm here." Molly took Ciara's hand and rubbed it. "You're cold as ice. Let's get some gloves for you."

"O-okay." Ciara shook herself. "Sorry to freak out on you."

"Hey, if you can't freak out with your favourite aunt, where can you?" Molly hugged Ciara. "Breathe deeply until your heart stops racing. You can get through this."

They wandered through the store looking for gloves for Ciara and winter boots for Molly. They couldn't find any boots, but Molly found a pair of funky ski gloves for Ciara. She paid for their purchases, and they headed back to the bus stop. The had to wait long enough to thoroughly test Molly's new coat.

At Aberdeen Mall they wandered aimlessly looking through the stores. The prices on the boots shocked Molly, most of them didn't look that warm either. Ciara bought a scarf to match her gloves. Molly found a pair of boots she didn't mind. The price was more than she expected, but why was she working if not to splurge once in a while? She paid for them before she could change her mind.

They found the food court and bought Chinese food to eat.

"Ciara!" A mob of girls and a couple of boys came over to her.

"Hi, I'm taking my aunt shopping."

"You're taking your aunt? Shouldn't it be the other way around?" One of the girls said.

"Ciara is much better at shopping than I am." Molly laughed, and a couple of the girls nodded.

"I saw Rebecca in that movie last night." Ciara grinned. "You know, my friend on facebook."

"Yeah, she's cool, how was the movie?" One of the boys asked.

"It broke me." Ciara took a deep breath. "Rebecca played the younger version of this grandmother who had been in the Residential Schools. We learned about them in school, but it never felt real until I saw the movie."

"Wow. Intense," the boy said. "Was it only on the one night?"

"I think it's on again tonight." Molly said and tapped on her phone. "Yep, same double bill as last night."

"Maybe mom will drive us." The boy looked at one of the girls.

"Probably, if we tell her it's for school." The girl grinned. "We could all go as a group."

"Even your little brother?" Another girl asked laughing.

"You have a problem with that? Matt is only a few minutes younger than me."

"Sorry, sorry," the other girl held up her hands. "Didn't mean to get under your skin. You're always teasing him about being the little brother."

"He's my brother, it's my job."

The group laughed and went on as if nothing had happened.

"The cops shot some guy near the movie theatre last night. Did you see anything?"

"Any blood?"

"It would be so cool if you saw it."

Ciara held up her hands to slow the flood of words as speculation ran wild through the group, but it didn't stop them.

"That's enough." The other boy stepped forward between Ciara and the others. "Death isn't cool."

The group hung their heads for a moment.

"Sorry, dude." The first boy said, and most of the girls nodded.

"Yeah Dean, we got carried away." The first boy's sister chimed in.

"Okay, we're good." Dean waved a hand. "It happens. You okay, Ciara?"

Ciara stepped up and wrapped her arms around Dean. "Thank you."

He stood stiff for a moment, then moved his arms to hold her. "That bad, huh? If you need to talk, just ask."

Ciara nodded her head and sniffled, then stepped back and wiped her eyes. "I will."

Dean nodded to her and looked like he didn't know what to do next.

"We'll let you know what we think of the movie." The girl twin reached a hand toward Ciara.

"Thanks, Misty." Ciara took the girl's hand for a moment. "I'd like that."

"See you at school." Dean didn't take his eyes away from Ciara.

"Yeah." Ciara reddened.

The mob moved on, making plans about the movie. Molly watched them as Ciara rubbed her eyes and pulled herself together.

"I like your friends." Molly put a hand on Ciara's shoulder.

"They're all right."

"Dean seems to be a bit more than all right."

"He's sort of my boyfriend." Ciara reddened further. "Don't tell Grandma, she'll just say I'm too young to have a boyfriend."

"My lips are sealed." Molly drew a finger across her mouth in a zipping motion. "But in return, if you ever need to talk about him, you call me."

"Sure Molly." Ciara heaved a sigh. "I think I need to go home now."

"Okay." Molly put an arm around Ciara's shoulder, "let's go catch a bus."

***

"We saw a bunch of Ciara's friends at the mall, it got a little intense." Molly explained as Ciara headed upstairs to her room.

"Oh?" Hanna put the kettle on to boil.

"They'd heard about the shooting, and since Ciara was in the area, they asked a lot of questions."

"Thank you for taking care of her."

"Actually, a young man named Dean stepped in."

Hanna shook her head. "That boy, his brother committed suicide and Dean found him. He was a handful for a time. Ciara's sweet on him, but she thinks I don't know."

"I'm not surprised." Molly took the mugs out. "It's like her closet, she needs privacy, but she also needs people."

"So Dean impressed you?"

"He did." Molly nodded as Hanna poured the tea.

"Maybe I'll wait a while before I discover Dean." Hanna sat and Molly took the chair across from her.

"I think they could be good friends." Molly sipped at her tea and took a cookie from the plate on the table.

"She's growing up so fast." Hanna shook her head. "I'm terrified she'll go down the same path as her mother."

"You're doing an amazing job raising her, trust the bond between you."

"Okay. I know she tells you things she'd never tell me, keep watching over her."

"I will." Molly cupped her hands around the mug and let the warmth relax her. "I'd better be thinking about heading home."

"Why don't you stay another night, I'm sure Blue won't mind." Hanna's eyes pleaded.

"Let me call Blue and let him know." Molly pulled her phone out and dialed. "Hey, Blue, I'm going to stay another night. Some stuff happened and Ciara needs me."

"Okay," Blue said, "I'll just warm up the stir fry."

"Thanks." Molly hung up. "I'm sure he worries about me; I worry about him. His job keeps him really busy, and it isn't what he wants to be doing."

"I'm guessing you're the same."

"I am, except I'm moving toward what I want, and Blue seems to be moving away."

"People change, life changes." Hanna shrugged. "We can't stop it, so we might as well enjoy the ride."

"I'll help you with supper." Molly got up. "I expect Ciara will come downstairs ravenously hungry."

Molly chopped vegetables while Hanna put a roast on to cook. It reminded Molly of cooking with Tad at the Café. *Why did I stop helping him cook? Well taking a full-time job probably has something to do with it.* She pushed the thoughts out of her head and concentrated on the veggies.

Ciara came down the stairs rubbing her eyes and asking what was for supper. She stopped and stared at Molly.

"I though you would have left already."

"You need me more than Blue right now. I can give you another night."

Ciara hugged her tight. "Thanks, Molly."

"You're family." Molly returned the hug. "Just as much as Blue."

Ciara nodded without letting go, then sighed and stepped back.

They ate supper, then watched a program on TV. Ciara sighed and snuggled up to Molly.

"Just for tonight, I'm going to be a little kid again."

***

Molly stared at the ceiling of Ciara's room. Ciara had insisted that Molly take the bed and she slept on a mat on the floor.

"Molly." Ciara whispered. "What's it like to be you?"

"I don't really know. I haven't been anyone else."

"Yes you have. You were a foster kid, then lived on the street and did drugs and had sex to make money. Then you went to school in Alberta and came back and were so cool. I wished you were my big sister the first time we met. Now you're a social worker and doing things to help people."

"All those people still live inside me." Molly turned on her side. "I take care of them so they don't jump out and make me hurt people. I keep growing but I don't stop being me."

"Can I tell you a secret?" Ciara rolled over and faced Molly. "I'm scared. Scared I'll make a mistake and hurt a bunch of people. Scared that I don't know what I'm doing. I like Dean, but I don't know if I really want a boyfriend."

"Dean can be a regular friend. He doesn't need to be a boyfriend."

"We kissed once." Ciara's voice dropped to where Molly had to struggle to hear her. "It was weird, not at all what I thought. What if I'm doing it wrong?"

"I've never really kissed someone." Molly reached down and took Ciara's hand. "I don't know how I'd feel if I did. But I'm not going to let the past me stop me from moving forward."

"But you..." Ciara tailed off, "...you know."

"I have, but never because I loved someone or wanted to. I don't know if I can love someone that way."

"That's sad." Ciara squeezed Molly's hand. "I'm sure you will find someone."

"I hope so." Molly's throat closed.

"Let's make a promise." Ciara gripped Molly's hand tightly. "We'll be the best us we can be, and maybe we can figure things out together."

"That's a promise." Molly used her other hand to wipe her eyes.

"Thanks, Molly." Ciara let go of Molly's hand and rolled over. "I'm glad you're my aunt."

"So am I." Molly rolled on her back. Ciara's breathing evened out. Molly sighed and closed her eyes and let sleep carry her away.

# CHAPTER 6
**Sunday November 21**

Ferguson stared at his notes. The interviews with the Bajwa family painted a picture of an ambitious business and family man. Hassim was checking out Bajwa's partners in ventures across Kamloops. Ferguson didn't expect to learn much, but it would give him another angle on the man.

The coroner had run the prints on the man involved in the officer involved shooting. He was Dennis Colm. Mr. Colm had several drunk and disorderlies and a couple of assault convictions. He'd be let off with time served and parole, then disappeared onto the street until the next time.

The officer who fired his gun insisted Colm had a knife, and there was a knife on the street. IIO had it currently. Ferguson picked up his phone and called the Independent Investigations Office.

"Hello Sergeant Ferguson with the Kamloops attachment. I'm inquiring about evidence from the officer involved shooting Friday night." He tapped his fingers while he was transferred to another person.

"Hello Sergeant..." He went through the same spiel and was transferred to another person.

This third person picked up.

"McCauley, IIO."

Ferguson explained again who he was and what he was looking for.

"What evidence?" McCauley said. "We can't release anything until the case is resolved."

"The knife on the scene of the shooting may be the murder weapon in a killing that happened just around the corner the same night."

"I see." McCauley didn't sound sympathetic. "I will see what I can do. Can I contact you at this number?"

"Yes. I appreciate your help."

"I haven't helped yet." McCauley hung up.

Ferguson stared at the phone and sighed. He'd done what he could. At least he had photos of the knife, maybe the Doc would be able to give him a hint from that. Bajwa's autopsy was tomorrow early. Ferguson printed a few pictures of the knife and put them in an envelope. All he could do was ask. While he waited, he'd dig deeper into Colm's background. Maybe there was something to find in the years before he'd showed up in Kamloops.

The national record on Colm began in Toronto, and slowly moved west as the man wore out his welcome in different jurisdictions. Colm had a sealed file which obscured his life before Toronto. Ferguson sent a note to the detachment commander. Accessing sealed files was beyond his pay grade.

Tomorrow would be a long day. He'd pack up for now and go home to rest.

***

Molly poured syrup over her pancakes and dug in. Ciara was still sleeping, and Hanna wanted her to rest as long as she could.

Hanna put a mug of tea beside Molly. "Penny for your thoughts."

"They don't make pennies anymore." Molly picked up her tea. "But I think you are overpaying. I'm thinking about how much I'm enjoying eating your pancakes."

Hanna laughed and sat across from Molly with her own mug of tea. "Dig a little deeper and I'll make it a nickel."

"Fine then," Molly stuffed a forkful of pancake into her mouth and thought as she chewed. "How do I encourage Ciara's freedom, but still guide her away from the dangerous paths?"

"You can't," Hanna sighed. "Freedom means the choice of the dangerous path needs to be there. All we can do is love her and show her examples of how to live well. She is alternating between a child and an almost adult. It's a scary time for her, and for us."

"I remember being that age, it wasn't pretty." Molly cut another bite.

"Your choices were limited by your circumstances, when your circumstances changed, your choices changed."

"I guess." Molly shook her head. "I certainly never had a group of friends like Ciara's."

"She doesn't talk about her friends much." Hanna sipped her tea, then added a bit more sugar. "I think she wants to protect them from her mean grandma. They are part of a separate world Ciara is part of where she's an equal and the rules are different."

"From what I saw of her friends, I like them." Molly went back to eating the pancakes.

"That's good to hear." Hanna rolled her shoulders. "As Ciara keeps telling me, I need to relax."

Molly laughed and continued eating.

"You talking about me?" Ciara came into the kitchen still in sleeping pants and t-shirt.

"Of course." Hanna grinned at her. "That's what grandmas and aunties do."

Ciara snorted and helped herself to a heap of pancakes and poured syrup on them. "What have you decided about me?"

"We agree that you are a very special young woman." Hanna peered at Ciara over the mug.

"Right." Ciara rolled her eyes. "Tell me another one."

"We love you." Molly leaned forward to catch Ciara's eyes. "You, not some image of a perfect Ciara we have in our heads, but occasionally we'll slip up and try to make choices for you."

"What kind of tea is that?" Ciara picked up Molly's mug and sniffed at it. "You must be on something."

"It's probably the syrup on the pancakes." Molly swabbed a piece of pancake in the syrup and ate it. Ciara laughed. "Is this a good time to ask to have a party here?"

"I think that is a good idea." Hanna said. "I would like to meet your friends. Molly was quite impressed by them."

"A party with boys too?" Ciara stared at her grandma.

"If you have boys you want to invite."

Ciara's jaw dropped. "Who are you and what did you do to my grandma?"

Molly snorted, then coughed on her tea.

"You are old enough to make some decisions for yourself." Hanna said. "The only way you will learn to make good decisions is by making choices and dealing with the consequences."

Ciara ate mechanically as Hanna raised a brow at Molly.

"Molly's a witness. You said I could have a party here. What if no one wants to come?" Ciara got a terrified look on her face.

"I can't imagine your friends passing up a party. Any parents who are reluctant can call me and we'll talk."

"What's a good date?" Ciara got the calendar from the fridge. "Not too close to Christmas, but close enough I can decorate the basement room."

"That room's a disaster, we'll have to work hard to make it ready for a proper party." Hanna said.

"We can start right after breakfast." Ciara shovelled more pancake into her mouth.

"Slow down, we have all day." Hanna patted Ciara's back. "Don't want to choke before your first party."

***

"How's Ciara and Hanna?" Blue asked as Molly came in the door.

"Busy cleaning out the basement room in preparation for a party. We discovered an entire couch Hanna had forgotten about under the boxes. Most of them were full of Ciara's grandfather's stuff, so it was half cleaning and half treasure hunt."

"Sounds like fun." Blue smiled at her.

"Dusty fun." Molly made a face. "I'm going to have a shower."

Once clean and in fresh clothes Molly sat down in the living room with Blue.

"We had a good time at the movie. The one with her friend in it really struck home. That would have been fine but then there was a police incident when we were leaving the theatre and Ciara almost saw a man being shot dead."

"Oh no, is she okay?" Blue leaned forward in his chair.

"A bit fragile at first, but she's bouncing back. Ciara knows she can talk to me anytime."

"She's a lucky girl to have someone like you in her life." Blue sighed and leaned back. "I saw the news. Apparently, the man who died may have murdered someone before confronting the police."

"That's terrible." Molly turned on the TV. "I want to see the six o'clock news."

"Find with me." Blue got up. "I'll do something about dinner while you watch."

The news people highlighted the murder victim. "Pathi Bajwa was a successful businessman in Kamloops, best known for his dealership. But he's been involved in several development projects. A suspect in the murder was shot by police. The Independent Investigation Office is studying the circumstances. The suspect was a person name Dennis Colm, of no fixed address. Anyone who may have information about the murder, or the shooting is asked to contact the police."

"I met him." Molly gaped at the TV. "He's the one who tried to pick a fight in the coffee shop on Tuesday. Then he came into work the next day. He didn't remember a thing about it. I should tell the police about it."

"Call and leave a message. If they think it's important, they'll get hold of you." Blue clattered about in the kitchen.

"I'll do that now." Molly pulled out her phone and looked up the non-emergency number for the Battle St. Station. "Hello, I just saw the news. The man who was shot who may have murdered someone. I met him a couple of times last week."

"I'll put you through to Sergeant Ferguson's voice mail. He will get in contact with you."

Molly repeated her statement on Sergeant Ferguson's voice mail, giving her name and phone number. Anxiety buzzed in her chest at the idea of talking to the Sergeant again. His name brought back some bad memories.

She breathed slowly to ease the tightness. Maybe he wouldn't think it important.

"Supper's on." Blue put a plate of fries and another of chicken wings on the table along with a bag of salad greens.

"Fancy." Molly sat down.

"Nothing but the best." Blue took his seat. "I thought sooner was better than fancy."

"I think you're right." She helped herself to fries and wings.

***

## Monday November 22

Armed with the print outs of the knife from the shooting scene, Ferguson entered the autopsy room.

The doc was already there setting up to record the autopsy. She nodded at Ferguson as he entered the room. Then introduced the video with the victim's name, the date, and who was present.

She examined the body describing any marks, or wounds.

"...a single wound to the thorax, no signs of struggle..." She made the Y incision and looked closely at the heart. This was done by someone who knew their way around knives. One sure blow to the left ventricle. There wasn't much blood on the clothes, so the knife was left in the wound until the victim died, then removed."

"Wouldn't that mean waiting over the body for a while?" Ferguson peered at the heart.

"Not necessarily." she pointed to the slash in the heart. "See how the wound is about the same length as the entry wound on the body. Whoever did this stabbed, then twisted the knife to open a larger cut. The blood pumped into the thoracic cavity making breathing impossible. Death would have been within minutes if not seconds."

"Pretty cold and calculated for someone who got himself shot by the police shortly afterward."

Ferguson pulled out the photos. "I wanted to ask if you think the wound is consistent with this knife?

She took the photos and laid them out on a table. "The general shape of the blade is right, the length is enough to reach the heart. I could be more specific if I could examine the knife itself.

"I'm working on that." Ferguson said.

The doc returned to the autopsy table and pointed to discolouration on the legs. "He was dead for a while, long enough for the blood to pool in his lower extremities. How long between the shooting and finding the body?"

"No more than fifteen minutes. He was found by an officer setting up the perimeter. The coroner arrived about an hour and a half after that."

"That would be quick for visible livor mortis in cold conditions, but not impossible." The doc shook her head. The cold would delay rigor mortis as well, making onset at least six hours after death."

She consulted her notes.

"What are you thinking?" Ferguson asked.

"There could be a significant delay between his death and the shooting. Rigor set in before the body reached the morgue, which would be quick for a warm day. I doubt the killer stabbed the victim, pulled the knife out after death, and went straight out to confront the police. I'm estimating the victim was dead at least two hours before he was found."

"So if Colm was the killer, what was he doing between killing the man and acting wildly on the street corner?"

"Are you sure that was the primary crime scene?" Doc stared off into space for a dozen breaths. "If the murder took place somewhere warm and the victim was moved to where he was found, it could explain the timeline."

"We found a shopping cart a bit farther down the alley. It is still being processed, but a body could be transported in one of those. Had a tarp covering it."

They finished the autopsy and Ferguson took off the PPE and headed to where they were processing the cart and its contents.

"Aside from the usual assortment." The lab tech waved at the contents laid out on a plastic sheet in a room in the basement. "We found three hundred in cash, mostly twenties. The Bajwa's wallet was present, all the cards were there, but no cash. There may have been a robbery. Another strange thing was a three-quarters empty bottle of vodka. It could explain the erratic behaviour on the street. It is a rather expensive brand for a street person to be drinking."

"Prints on the bottle?" Ferguson asked,

"Most of them belong to Colm."

"Most of them?" Ferguson raised an eyebrow.

"A few unidentified prints. They don't match the victim. For all we know they could belong to the salesperson who put the bottle in the bag."

"Did you find a bag?"

"Dozens of them, some from liquor stores."

"Any receipts. Was vodka Colm's booze of choice?"

"Haven't found any yet. None of the other bottles in the cart were vodka, but he could have picked them up. Had a lot of cans too."

"Anything that might indicate a body was transported in the thing?"

"Nothing yet." The tech made a note. "We'll have a close look for fibres."

"Great, thanks." Ferguson nodded and climbed the stairs to his desk. The blinking light saying he had a message blinked at him. He pushed the play button

A familiar voice informed him she might have information about Dennis Colm, it wasn't until she gave her name and number that he recognized Callister's voice. The woman had an instinct for trouble. He dialed Callister's number. She answered on the first ring.

"Molly here."

"You left a message for me? Are you at home and able to talk?"

"I have a few minutes before I leave for work. I'll call in and say I might be late."

He called Hassim and asked her to meet him at the car. Then headed down to the parking lot.

"Got a lead?" Hassim fastened her seatbelt and started the car.

"A phone call from Molly Callister." Ferguson replied. "She's lives on the North Shore on Fortune St."

"Got it." Hassim turned onto Sixth and headed for Lansdowne.

Ferguson pulled out his phone and called Callister. "Ferguson here, we should be there in a few minutes."

"I'll meet you at the doors."

Callister stood arms crossed in the lobby. She opened the door for them and led them up to her apartment and invited them in.

"I was out with a friend last Tuesday. Dennis Colm came into the coffee shop and tried to pick a fight." She went on to describe the incident. "Strange thing was he came into my work the next day and didn't recognize me."

"You still have the knife you took from Colm?" Hassim asked.

Callister stood and fetched it from a coat pocket and handed it to Ferguson.

"He looked like he was having trouble opening it when he dropped it."

"I'll have the lab took at it." Ferguson dropped it into an evidence bag and put it in a pocket

"Thank you for your help." Ferguson closed his notebook. He followed Hassim out of the apartment. "What do you think?"

"I think she was reporting on an incident like a good citizen. It would be stretching things to suggest she has anything else to do with the case."

"I agree." Ferguson put his hands in his pockets. "Let's find out who did the follow up and read the report."

# CHAPTER 7
## Monday November 22

Molly read the news on her break. Pathi Bajwa's murder and the shooting of Dennis Colm were making a big splash. She'd heard the talk on the street while checking out her clients. In the mind of the public at least, Colm was a crazed killer and got no more than he deserved. What concerned her was the underlying fear mongering about the homeless in general.

The incident at the coffee shop bothered her, not so much because of Colm's demand for a fight, but that Tad had seemed ready to give him one. She didn't know anything about Tad, other than they shared an interest in movies. Most of their conversations were about movies, not their lives. Her clients were more familiar to her than her friend.

The sight of Trenchcoat Guy crossing the road ahead distracted her from her thoughts. She picked up her pace to intersect him.

"Hi Edwin." Molly smiled at him. "Do you remember seeing me at the office?"

"I do, you gave me that marvelous map." He looked around. "It is very valuable information. I will keep it safe." Scanning the street again, he straightened his coat. "I must be going."

Molly watched him walk along the street. He had the look of perpetual alertness that she remembered from her days on the street. Living rough was no picnic. A disturbance ahead caught her attention. Three men were yelling at a homeless man.

"We don't want you here."

"All of you should be in jail."

Their target scowled at them and swore, which only egged the men on.

"Is there a problem?" Molly asked which pulled the attention of the three men to her and allowed the homeless man to escape.

"Yeah, the streets are crawling with that filth. Somebody should do something about them."

"You're volunteering?" She raised an eyebrow.

"What it to you? You one of those people who think we should coddle criminals?" The biggest man stepped up into Molly's face.

"It isn't a crime to be poor." Molly met his gaze and refused to back down.

The man grabbed the front of her coat and twisted to choke her. He ignored the comments from others on the street, and his buddies kept watch.

"It is a crime to assault someone." Molly spoke evenly through the heat that raged through her body. Several plans of escape jumped into her mind, but she resisted the temptation to use the self defense skills she'd added to her judo since returning to Kamloops. Escalating the situation would do nothing to help anyone. She didn't want to get any bystanders hurt. "You're setting a bad example for anyone watching."

"Well, shoot, I wouldn't want to do that now." The man holding her grinned maliciously and clenched his fist.

"What is going on here?" Constable Post stepped out of an unmarked car and frowned.

"You idiots were supposed to be keeping watch." The man pushed Molly back and she fell into a fighting stance, wanting to release a load of pain on this jerk.

"We've been getting complaints about people starting fights." Post frowned at the man.

"Just doing your job for you." The man turned to walk away, but Post caught him and pushed him against the car. "Spread your legs hands behind your head."

"You getting this? Police overreaching their authority." He looked around for his two friends, but they'd vanished, and the crowd muttered ominously.

The man's smug look faded. "You can't hold me for anything. I know my rights."

"We'll start with assault and public mischief." Post hand cuffed the man and sat him in the car. "You clowns are on more than one security camera. Ms. Callister, are you okay, you need anything?"

"Fine, Constable Post." Molly straightened herself. "If you need to talk to me, you know where to find me."

Post stepped closer to Molly and dropped his voice. "Just what do you think you were doing?"

"I intervened when they were threatening a homeless man. I didn't expect it to escalate."

"So, you were going to stand there and let him hit you?" Post frowned.

"Wouldn't be the first time I've taken a beating." Molly snorted "And I didn't want to hurt him. That would cause more trouble than a black eye."

Post shook his head. "You don't go looking for trouble, but it does have a habit of finding you." He climbed into the car and drove away.

The crowd dispersed and Molly sighed and fought off the shakes from the end of the adrenaline rush. She scanned the street but didn't see any of her clients. Most of them were too smart stick around confrontations. She would walk down to the Overlander Bridge and see if anyone was hanging out.

***

Molly checked in with the office and wrote up her reports, keeping her description of the altercation carefully neutral. After that she headed home. Normally she only kept a weather eye out for trouble, but this evening she scanned the street constantly and arrived at the apartment exhausted.

Blue looked up from the news on TV. "Rough day?"

"You could say that." Molly opened the oven to check on the casserole. "Chicken Divan, good choice. I'm going to have a shower. See you in a few."

The hot water washed away the last of the day. She put her pajamas and a robe on and went out to the kitchen.

"Anything you want to talk about?" Blue looked up from setting the table.

"Just some asses trying to cause trouble." Moll took diner out of the over and set it on a trivet. "Let's eat."

They sat down and ate in silence. Blue kept eyeing her and almost saying something.

"What's up?" Molly put her fork down. "You keep looking at me like you're expecting me to break."

"Something on the news while you were in the shower. Reports of street people being intimidated. There was a video."

"Damn, just what I need." Molly barely kept from banging the table. "Any time there's trouble, some people have to go after the poorest and weakest."

"And other people stand up for them." Blue sighed and rubbed his temples. "I know you can take care of yourself, but I'm still worried. It only takes one stab with a knife and everything changes."

"I know." Molly dropped her voice. "I know. I worry about the same thing. But it is worse to do nothing and be afraid someone else will get hurt."

"I understand." Blue sighed. "It doesn't make it any easier."

"I hear you." Molly stared at her plate. "If it makes you happier, I am not looking for trouble, but as Constable Post told me, it finds me anyway."

"That it does." Blue leaned forward. "I'm worried, but I'd be more worried if you retreated from the world and did nothing."

Molly opened her mouth to respond, but her phone rang.

"Hello."

"Ms. Callister what is your reaction to the video of you circulating through the community?" A young woman's voice asked.

"You're doing your part to help the circulation." Molly relaxed her shoulders. "I haven't seen the video in question, but I can guess what it shows. Everyone needs to do what they can to stop violence. That can mean calling the police, taping an incident."

"Or standing up to the bully?" The woman asked. "What went through your head when he was holding you?"

"The blaming of all people on the street for the possible actions of one is just one more way for us to avoid the reality of our failure."

"Failure?"

"The weakest and poorest among us didn't choose their lives. As long as we continue to look away and refuse to see our responsibility, we are to blame."

"Thank you for talking with me." The woman hung up, and Molly dropped her head into her hands.

"That's going to play well with the boss."

"True enough." Blue nodded and came around the table to hug her. "But the truth is rarely popular."

"I don't want to get fired over this." Molly leaned her head back against Blue's chest.

"If you get fired for telling the truth, the job isn't right for you."

"I guess." Molly's phone rang again. "Hello."

"Ms. Callister as a former candidate for major what is your reaction to the increased violence on the streets?" A man asked.

"We are too quick to assign blame for violence and crime." Molly said. "And I wasn't a candidate."

"You don't think people should be held accountable?"

"Accountability should come through the court system, not by a few good old boys looking for the marginalized to beat up."

"Right." The man stayed silent, probably trying to think of another question. Molly hung up. The phone rang immediately.

"What?" Molly growled into the phone.

"What's wrong, Molly?" Tad said. "Are you okay?"

"Sorry, just being hounded for comments about the video of me standing up to a bully."

"I saw that." Tad sounded strange. "I'm sorry I wasn't there to protect you."

"I don't want to be protected, Tad. I'm not a fragile china doll. I need a friend more than I need a bodyguard."

"I see." Tad's voice shook. "I won't bother you anymore."

Molly glared at the phone, tempted to phone him back and rant, but that wouldn't help anything. Instead, she turned the phone off. "I'm going to bed."

"You that tired?" Blue sounded concerned.

"No, I just don't want to deal with anything else tonight."

"Okay," Blue said, "I'm here if you need me."

***

Molly woke up groggy in the middle of the night but couldn't fall asleep. Tad had sounded so hurt, she hadn't meant to hurt him, but the notion that he saw himself as her protector bothered her. It wasn't that she didn't like the idea of someone to back her up at need, but she wondered if that was the only way Tad saw himself. She'd never asked him to guard her. Did she really need guarding? *I'm not that helpless.*

She rolled over and tried to put the whole thing out of her mind, but thoughts chased themselves in circles and kept her awake. Finally, she got up and fired up her computer. Might as well see what kind of nonsense the media was spouting about her. She was sure it would come up at work in the morning.

The video showed the man holding her coat, then panned to her face. It didn't show any emotion at all. None of the anger she felt, no fear, perhaps a mild annoyance that this person was interrupting her day.

*Do I really look like that?* Molly pulled up the video from the mayor's all candidates meeting. She forced herself to watch. Maybe she had more emotion there, but most of it was in her voice and words. Maybe she'd ask Blue later. Maybe.

She was ready to go back to bed and force herself to sleep, but the computer pinged, and a message popped up.

[ You're up late, or early.] Her grandmother in Alberta had sent.

[ Couldn't sleep.] Molly typed.

[ After the day you had, I'm not surprised.]

[?]

[ Blue called me for advice.]

Annoyance bloomed in Molly, but she took her hands away from the keyboard.

[ Seems you ran into a spot of trouble. He sent me the video.]

Molly rolled her eyes.

[ It was just some goons trying to cause trouble.] Molly ground her teeth.

[ He doesn't doubt you can take care of yourself, but he's worried he'll do the wrong thing.]

[ It's not like I don't make mistakes.]

[ We all do, but we don't enjoy it. Blue feels it more than most.]

[ I guess.]

[ Either we externalize the blame, or we take it on ourselves.]

[ It isn't his fault.]

[ True, but he feels responsible. There are always unintended consequences to every action.]

[ I know, but he shouldn't blame himself. Stuff happens.]

[ True enough. Take care of each other.]

[ I'll try Grandmother.]

[ You need to talk, I'm here. I love you both.]

Her grandmother went offline, and Molly stared at the screen until her eyes blurred. She wiped them off, then put her computer to sleep and yawned. Crawling back into bed, Molly fell asleep almost immediately.

***

The voices bothered Hank. He hadn't had a drink in a while to silence them.

"Go away. Leave me alone. I'll kill you." It didn't matter what he said or threatened, they refused to shut up. He shook his head and waved his arms. They'd kept him up late and got him kicked out of the shelter. It was too fucking cold to sleep rough, so he staggered under the bridge and looked for anything that might give him relief from the chill and wind.

"Hey you." Another voice intruded. This one wasn't in his head, so Hank ignored it.

"I'm talking to you. A hand grabbed his shoulder and Hank swung wildly to knock it away. A blow landed on his stomach. Hank turned at tried to find his tormentor, but the voices made it so hard. Another fist struck his temple. He stumbled, the voices momentarily silent, and he spotted his opponent and tried to punch the man. "Trying to fight me?" The man shoved Hank. He stepped back into space and tumbled down the slope. Hank slammed into a rock and the breath whooshed out of his lungs. Pain replaced it. Hank tried to get up, get away, but his body failed him.

"Stay away from decent people." The voice floated down to Hank, but it was lost in the cacophony in his mind. He put his hands to his head, but the voices wouldn't stop.

Hank shivered against the rock, but his limbs wouldn't obey him, they flailed about, bruising against the rocky ground and opening a cut on his knuckles. The cold invaded him and sapped his strength. The voices screamed victoriously, but Hank closed his eyes and escaped them by falling into sleep.

# CHAPTER 8
## Tuesday November 23

"In the news this morning." The radio host said. "Molly Callister, known from the civic election last year, stepped in to stop the harassment of a street person. Our question for the next hour is. What about the homeless, are they victims of an uncaring system or addicts and criminals? Here's our first caller. Hello Stan."

"We need to clean up the streets." Stan spoke in staccato bursts. "Our crime is through the roof. If we give out free food and housing it will only encourage the addicts."

Bob had a relaxed cultured tone. "Nothing is free, the taxpayers are already carrying a heavy burden, why should be pay for people who don't want to work?"

"The whole homeless system is already costing us more than it would to give people food and housing and pay for supports to help them reconnect with the community." Annie rattled off her words as if expecting to be cut off.

"Molly Callister said, and I quote. 'The weakest and poorest among us didn't choose their lives. As long as we continue to look away and refuse to see our responsibility, we are to blame.' What about it? We live in one of the wealthiest countries in the world. Why are there still homeless people?"

The radio host stirred the pot before answering the next caller.

"We should bring in the army and round them all up." Jeff suggested. "It isn't the problem of hard-working people."

"Where would you put them after you've rounded them up?" The host asked.

"I don't know, Vancouver maybe. Anywhere but Kamloops."

"I drive down the Tranquille corridor every day, and every day I see people splayed on the sidewalk, trying to survive another day. It breaks my heart that we don't do more for them." Yvonne said.

The show continued with callers blaming the homeless for their own problems outweighing those who saw a community issue.

***

Don called her into his office

"You've become something of a celebrity." He waved her to a chair.

"I'm sorry if I've caused you any trouble." Molly looked down.

"Nothing more than usual." Don said. "But I would like you to view the video module on media relations, then come back and talk to me."

"Okay." Molly stood slowly. Don had gone back to his paperwork, so she went to the video room and found the tape in question. It was as dull as she'd expected, but she watched it twice in an attempt to discover what Don wanted her to learn. She wasn't a media liaison.

Molly froze. She wasn't a media liaison, but she'd made statements that could be construed to come from Streetreach, since she was their employee. Her answers to the reporters last night could be taken out of context and cause trouble. The agency stayed out of politics, preferring to advocate in the background.

She'd been told her first day of work, her job was to advocate for her clients, not to fix them, or their lives. Molly sighed and put the tape away and went back to Don's office.

"I think I've got it." Molly sat down and tried to sort out her thoughts. "I'm not the media liaison, so I need to be more aware of what I'm saying and how it could be twisted."

"You may need to make it clear that you are speaking for yourself, if you are asked how our agency sees the issue."

"Right." Molly took a deep breath. "Sorry for the trouble."

"You are young and passionate about issues, that's good, but it is also good to be aware of how your passion could be taken out of context to cause you damage."

"I will, thanks Don." Molly stood and Don nodded at her to go. She escaped the room with a sigh that it hadn't been worse.

She put her coat, hat, and gloves on and headed out. Today she was assigned to check on people sleeping under the overlander. The winter shelters were late and inadequate. The arguments were about who was to blame, not about how to fix the problem.

The walk along Tranquille and over the bridge had her shivering even with the new warmer coat and sweater she wore beneath it. It would get colder later in the winter, but she never felt it the same way as the first onset of the negative temperatures.

She hadn't seen any clients on her walk. They would be all at the Loop getting warm. Lucky them. Molly walked under the bridge and looked for a place to pick her way down the steep slope. A dirty blue bundle lay against a rock halfway down the hill. It wasn't moving. With a sinking feeling, Molly scrambled down the slope to the man and checked his pulse. Nothing. She quickly pulled her glove back on, then had to remove it to get to her phone and dial 911.

The ambulance and the police arrived at the same time, Fire and Rescue followed soon after to bring the poor man's body up the steep hill. Molly described how she'd found the body, hugging herself to try to warm up.

"You'd better get inside and warm up," the paramedic said as she closed the back door of the ambulance. Molly nodded. The police told her she could leave, so she climbed the slope and headed for the Café to warm up. She wouldn't be any good to anyone with her teeth chattering.

A cup of coffee and bowl of soup helped chase away the chill. Molly checked in with people at the Café. A crowd filled the place leaving her sitting at a corner of a table.  The Trenchcoat Guy sat on another corner.

"You staying warm, Edwin?" Molly spooned up a mouthful of soup.

"It is a challenge." Edwin sighed. "I do need to stay out of sight."

"Must be hard." Molly leaned back and gazed at him. "Staying away from everybody."

"One gets used to it in time." Edwin looked down, then finished eating his soup.

"I don't know if I could do it." Molly imagined her life without Blue, Ciara, even Tad, and had to take a long breath to stop her throat from closing up.

"I hope you never have to." Edwin got up and put his hat on. "Take care." He left her with a nod. Molly ate her meal, then knocked on Blue's office door.

"Come in." Blue called.

Molly walked in and closed the door behind her. She sat in a chair and heaved a sigh.

"Tough day?" Blue put his pen down and looked at her.

"Found a man frozen to death this morning, then had a conversation about isolating oneself from the world. It was sad." Molly stared at her feet.

"That is sad." Blue's chair squeaked as he swung back and forth. "You hear from Tad?"

"No, why?"

"He didn't come in for his shift at the Loop this morning. I was hoping you'd been talking to him."

"Nothing since the other night." Molly shook her head and took a ragged breath. "I wasn't trying to hurt him."

"We rarely do." Blue came around his desk to put a hand on Molly's shoulder. "If is any comfort, I agree that you don't need a bodyguard."

"I thought he respected me more." Molly dashed tears from her eyes. "I'm not just someone he needs to babysit."

"Agreed." Blue gave her a squeeze, then returned to his chair. "Either he will learn, or he won't. You can't take responsibility for his issues."

"I liked him." Molly whispered. "He was easy to be with."

"Someone who is always easy to be with is hiding their rough edges."

"Yeah." Molly stood up. "I'd better get on my way again. I still need to check the south riverbank if I want to get paid."

"Be careful." Blue picked up his pen. "I will see you at supper."

"Sure thing."

***

Hassim closed the tab on her browser. Pathi Bajwa had kept himself busy. He had been involved in several development deals. As far as she could tell, they were all straight forward and successful. Nothing that would be a motive for his murder. She read through Ferguson's notes from the autopsy and the work so far on the shopping cart.

Three hundred was a lot of cash for someone like Dennis Colm to be carrying around. It wasn't made up of scrounged bills, but a roll of twenties. Maybe they were missing the obvious. She called Rutvi Bajwa.

"Hello, Sergeant Hassim here. I have a quick question for you. How much cash did your husband usually carry?"

"Pathi didn't like cash, he said it was just asking for trouble. But he occasionally carried some depending on who he was going out with. "

"So it would be possible for him to have three hundred in twenties in his pocket?"

"It would be rare, but not impossible. Some of his partners like to flash rolls of cash and Pathi wanted to fit into their culture."

"Thanks for the help." Hassim hung up and sat deep in thought. Callister had handed them the knife she'd taken from Colm on Tuesday. Sometime between then and Friday he'd acquired another one. The one Callister turned in was a locking folding knife, the knife most likely used in the murder was a fixed blade kitchen knife. It looked cheap in the photo, like the ones the grocery stores sold with the plastic sheath included.

She called the lab people. "That cart you are cataloging, have you found any plastic sheaths for storing kitchen knives?"

"We've found all sorts of strange stuff, but I don't recall seeing that. Hold on."

Hassim listened to the flipping of paper as the tech looked through the list.

"Found it, black plastic holder." The tech said. "You might be interested to learn we found a receipt for the vodka bottle. Paid for with a debit card."

"Thanks, that's helpful."

"We're almost done."

"I'll come down and check it out as soon as you give us the word."

"Oh, almost forgot. You asked about any evidence the vic had been in the cart. We didn't find any fibres or the like, but there's a dark stain on the back of the victim's coat. Could have come from half a dozen things in the cart."

"Awesome." Hassim hung up and thought for a moment. Where would Colm get a cheap kitchen knife? He probably stole it. It was a long shot, but she checked for complaints from Wednesday to Friday last week. The only likely thing that came up was a call about a shoplifter. An officer had gone and taken a statement, but the video wasn't clear enough to pursue the case.

She texted Ferguson and headed over to the store.

"About time you got here." The manager crossed his arms over his substantial stomach. "The first guy they sent was useless." He led Hassim to a cramped office where he tapped at a computer and brought up video looking through the store.

The grainy image showed a man in a dark ball cap shuffling down an aisle. He scanned the area, then snatched something from the shelf. The manager skipped ahead to a repeat performance.

"The man's a habitual." He tapped his finger on the screen. I could show you going back months."

"Would you be able to send me the footage?"

"Can do better than that." The manager foraged around on the desk and came up with a thumb drive. We're going to ban him, but legal likes us to have hard evidence. Here's video of him going back three months." He handed it to Hassim."

"This will be very helpful." Hassim made a note and put the drive in her pocket. "I'll get it back to you when I'm done with it."

"Take your time." The manager waved a hand. "I know where it is if I need it, but I'm going to ban his ass." He showed Hassim a printout of a slightly fuzzy photo of the man in the black hat.

She checked her phone and pulled up the pictures of Colm on the street. She flipped through and compared them to the printout. "Good news." Hassim took the printout. "I don't think he'll be bothering you anymore."

"You going to arrest him?" The manager's face lit up.

"He's dead." Hassim said and the manager paled. "Nothing to do with your case, but you've been very helpful. Thank you."

"Any time."

Hassim texted Ferguson again and suggested they meet and go over the new evidence.

***

Ferguson thumbed through the autopsy report from Dennis Colm. It had come through the internal mail with a note saying the IIO was just about done their investigation and the evidence would be released to the Kamloops detachment when the report was finalized.

Colm had died from three gunshots to the torso. One of them had nicked his portal artery and he'd bled out in less than a minute. His blood alcohol level was absurdly high. Ferguson didn't know how the man could stay on his feet, never mind be a sufficient threat to warrant deadly force. Good thing that wasn't his problem. It did explain where that vodka had gone to. His phone buzzed. Hassim wanted to meet and talk about the case. Ferguson slid the autopsy report back into its envelope and carried it with him to Hassim's desk. He'd pick up coffees on the way.

Hassim spun away from her desk to face him, her face like a cat that ate the canary.

"You have something." Ferguson put her coffee on the desk beside her and sat down.

"We can put the knife in Colm's hands before Friday." Hassim showed him the thumb drive plugged into her computer and clicked through the files. She opened on showing Colm frowning as he walked past a camera, hands in his pockets. "Seems like Colm is a consistent shoplifter. Here's a video of him stealing something."

"Is that a knife?" Ferguson leaned forward and peered at the screen. Hassim clicked the mouse a few times and the image cleared up sufficiently for him to see it was a knife in plastic packaging.

"Just boosted the contrast and sharpened the image." Hassim tapped the screen. "The manager of the store called in a complaint. A constable responded but couldn't do much. That was Saturday, the time stamp on the video says it is from Thursday evening."

"Nice." Ferguson said. "Don't know that it would stand up in court, but that's looking less and less like an issue."

"Talked to the victim's wife. She said it would be unusual, but not impossible for Bajwa to carry three hundred in cash. Depended on who he was meeting. Techs found a receipt for the vodka from earlier, paid by debit card which matches one in Bajwa's wallet. Uncovered a plastic sheath from a cheap kitchen knife the same brand as the store Colm stole from." She opened a photo of the knife lying beside Colm. "Looks like a decent match to the weapon Colm was waving."

"McCauley from IIO sent over a copy of the autopsy on Colm. He must have chugged a good bit of that vodka. He was off the scales drunk." Ferguson handed her the envelope

"We know from Callister that Colm looks for fights when he's drunk." Hassim grinned. "We have Colm on the spot, put the weapon in his hand, and the motive looks like robbery."

"Why would he kill the man, stuff him in the cart, only to dump him in the alley and leave the cart in that same alley?" Ferguson scowled at the computer. "Doesn't make sense."

"He bumps into Bajwa and decides to rob him. Bajwa doesn't cooperate and gets stabbed. Colm won't want to leave the body on the street, so tips the body into the car and covers it with the tarp. First thought is to get the body out of the light, hence the alley. He dumps the corpse and takes the knife back but gets distracted by the vodka and drinks himself stupid until something sets him off." Hassim said. "Crime of the moment. It doesn't need to make sense."

"It does hang together." Ferguson nodded. "Let's run it past the Inspector, if he signs off on it, we're done. Something else. The brass turned up the fact that Colm had been military. The record was sealed as part of a plea deal."

"He could be good with a knife then. Callister was luckier than she knows." Hassim sipped her coffee, made a face, then drank the rest of it. "I'll set up a meeting with the Inspector. Then we're on to the next thing."

***

Molly sat on the couch; blanket pulled close around her. She couldn't concentrate on the TV program. It hadn't surprised her that Tad hadn't buzzed her to let her know he was here to go to the Tuesday movie with her. It did surprise her how much it hurt. The movie night had become a part of her life and the space it once filled was a jagged hole in her chest. If Tad called, she didn't know if she'd cry or scream at him. Maybe a bit of both. She pulled out her phone and dialled Tad. Once again, she got the message that the number was no longer in service.

Blue sat in the armchair half watching the TV half reading something, probably from work. She didn't mind that he wasn't paying attention to her. He was present. All she needed to do was speak up and he'd put the papers down and listen.

Only she couldn't think of what she'd say if he did turn to give her his full attention. Was she sad at losing a friend or angry at learning he didn't care about her, only about being a 'man' and protecting her? Her fist clenched. She had worried about him, lost sleep over whether she was being fair, and he

90

couldn't be bothered to break it off honestly. Shit, she was such an idiot. She buried her face in her knees and gasped to fight back the sobs.

The cushions on the couch moved and arms wrapped around her. Molly gave up the battle and let the tears flow. Blue didn't say anything, just held her until the storm passed.

"I wish I could do more." Blue tightened his grip.

"This is what I need." Molly leaned into his hug. "Thank you."

After the ache in her chest eased, Molly turned off the TV and went to bed. The world would continue turning and she had to be at work in the morning.

***

Wendy fumbled with the needle. She needed the fix, but her hand shook so much she was having trouble.

"Disgusting." A man's voice sneered at her.

"Fuck off." Wendy kept trying to get the needle into the vein in her arm.

"Here, let me help." Rough hands snatched the precious drug from her and stabbed it into her neck. The high hit hard and she rolled on her back laughing. Her heart slowed as the universe spun around her. She didn't notice when it stopped.

# CHAPTER 10
## Wednesday November 24

Molly poured herself another cup of coffee and tried to get her head on straight. She'd woke up grumpy and deliberately hid in her room until Blue left for work. Talking with anybody would be a mistake. Meditating while sipping her coffee wasn't the best, but she didn't have time to do them separately.

An ambulance pulled out from behind the agency as she walked up. No siren, so either the person had recovered or died. She hoped for the first, but her gut told her it was the second. Pushing through the door, Molly headed for the briefing.

"Good morning, Molly." Don glanced up at her as she sat at the table. "You okay?"

"Okay enough." Molly leaned forward. "Sorry I didn't get much done yesterday."

"Not surprising, finding a body is always a shock to the system. I would be concerned if you went through the rest of your day without a reaction."

"I guess." She played with her pen.

"I saw your report on your conversation with Edwin." Don smiled slightly. "The Trench Coat Guy as some of you call him. I think that's the most anyone has got from him."

"All I said was it must be lonely." Molly doodled and didn't look up.

"Exactly, you empathized with him without offering solutions. Don't underestimate the power of just listening."

"Yes." Molly shook her head. "Sorry, I'm in a bad mood today."

"We all have days like that."

The other workers arrived, and Don scanned the room. His eyes paused on Molly, but he didn't say anything.

"We've lost two people to the cold." He opened the meeting. "In both situations the workers who found the body acted properly, but I am going to go over the procedure just as a refresher."

Molly forced herself to listen carefully, it distracted her from her mood. Helen rubbed her eyes and Molly guessed she'd found the person behind the agency.

"Helen will work out of the office today. Some of you have appointments, be sure to take your client somewhere warm to talk. Both the Loop and the Café have space for you to meet with clients. Molly, I'd like you to take River Walk along Schubert. Community Services told us there are still a few people camped there. See if you can help them find better shelter, even if it is only a warm place during the day. I don't want any more bodies on the street."

"Yes, Don." Molly nodded sharply. Her mood would have to wait until work was done. The others were sent out downtown and along Tranquille. They had a team around Sahali who worked out of a van outfitted like a mobile office. Molly would love to work with them, but she couldn't drive. Maybe that should be the next item on her self-improvement list. Helen had people talking to her, so she gathered up her messenger bag and coat and got ready to go out in the cold. At least it wasn't snowing.

"Molly, you want to walk with me along Tranquille?" Ben stood at her elbow. "I'd like to talk with you."

"Okay." Molly kept her sigh internal. Ben didn't deserve the fallout from her grumps. They stepped out the door and walked south.

"I don't know if I could handle finding a dead person." Ben didn't look at her.

"It was more sad than scary." Molly adjusted her bag. "Better me than a member of the public. We have a team to back us up."

"I found my grandma when I was a kid. It terrified me. I didn't sleep in the dark for years."

"You were a kid. It would be scary, especially someone you knew well."

"I still have a phobia about bodies. I can't even go to funerals if there is an open casket."

"Our coping skills stay with us until they no longer work." Molly looked around at the street, not very busy with the cold weather. "Mine was to not trust anyone but myself, and not even that at times."

"Sounds lonely," Ben said. "How did you change?"

"Very slowly." Molly laughed and looked over at Ben. "And I had a lot of help. Don't try to do it by yourself."

"Right." Ben pointed across the street. "There's Astrid, I'd better go see how her search for shelter is going. Thanks for listening."

Maybe he was as scared of change as of bodies. Molly didn't blame him. Change was hard. She watched him dodge traffic, then put him out of her mind.

She reached the Overlander Bridge and walked under it. A couple people huddled away from the wind. Molly headed their way.

"It's warm at the Loop."

"Don't like that place." The older man grumbled. "Don't let me bring my dog in."

"Your dog is the meanest thing this side of Hell." The other said. "Why do you think I always keep you between him and me?"

"A man needs a mean dog to survive."

"Even if you can't go inside, they will give you a warm meal to go." Molly said.

"Nah, don't need anyone's sympathy." The old one shoved the other. "You go if you want, wuss."

"Not while you have the weed." He moved to shove back, and the dog growled. Molly hadn't noticed it until then. It sat inside the man's coat only eyes and teeth showing.

"Take care of yourselves then." Molly continued her walk, making notes on her phone.

The others she found weren't any more receptive to her invitation. They had well camouflaged camps and eyed her mistrustfully.

"You going to report us to Community Services?" One got in her face.

"No, they know you're here. They asked me to check on you." Molly stepped back and raised her hands.

The woman frowned and stared at Molly. "Leave me alone." She turned and stomped back to her camp.

"You have to excuse her." A young man wrung his hands. "She's been through a lot of rough stuff."

"I understand." Molly handed him a card. "Call if you need help."

He took the card, looking over his shoulder.

"Jack, you get your ass down here." The woman shouted and Jack paled.

"You'd better go." Molly nodded to him and left.

The rest of her day wasn't much different. Some talked her ear off; others swore at her. She swung past the Safeway and North Hills Mall on her way back and walked into the office to grab a coffee and write up her reports. She'd barely warmed up before it was time to head home.

Blue hadn't made it home yet, probably caught up in a meeting. Molly didn't envy him. She put a casserole in the oven then took a shower to get rid of the last of the chill.

She'd missed a call while in the shower. Ciara left her a message begging her to call.

"Hi Ciara, what can I do for you?"

"Grandma and I have been planning the party. What if no one comes?"

"That is a scary thought." Molly checked the casserole, then sat on the couch. "I've never thrown a party, so I don't know much about it."

"You've been to parties." Ciara asked. "What did you do?"

"You don't want that kind of party." Molly put a hand to her head. "Trust me." The thought of Ciara experiencing her life sent a spike of pain through her.

"That's no help." Ciara said and hung up.

Molly staggered to the bathroom and threw up. She was rinsing her mouth when Blue came through the door. She tried to tell Blue what happened, but she was shaking too much. Sitting on the couch she focused on her breathing until she lost awareness of everything but the pain and fear. She stared them in the face and refused to budge. How many times would she have to do this? *At least one more time than it happens.* The panic faded and exhaustion set in. She leaned over and put her head on the arm of the couch and closed her eyes.

***

Blue tucked a blanket around Molly and turned the oven off. He'd had enough panic attacks to recognize one.

It didn't make it any easier to watch.

She woke up about an hour later. "Supper!"

"It's all right, I turned the oven off." Blue crouched down to look her in the eyes. "You feeling better?"

"Not really." Molly pushed herself to sitting position and tugged the blanket tight around her. "Ciara called about the party she's planning with Hanna; I think I disappointed her. I know nothing about anything a thirteen year old should be at."

"That's tough one." Blue looked up at the ceiling. "I don't know much more, but I can guess who does."

"Grandmother?" Molly perked up and looked for her phone. Blue brought it to her. She dialed quickly and froze, phone to her ear. "Hi Grandmother, it's Molly. Can you give me a call when you have a chance?" She hung up and dropped the phone beside her.

Blue stood up and fetched the casserole out of the oven. "Dinner's ready if you have any appetite."

"I'll eat a little." Molly moved to a kitchen chair, still with the blanket wrapped around her. Blue served up two plates and put one in front of Molly along with a glass of water. She started by picking at the food but ending up eating it all and a bit more.

"That's better." Blue collected the dishes, rinsed them, and put them in the dishwasher.

Molly's phone rang and she jumped up to answer it. "Hi Hanna." She pushed the blanket aside. "What can I do for you?" She put the phone on speaker.

"Ciara is having a tantrum." Hanna said over the sound of swearing in the background. "Something about forgetting about the party, and it's a stupid idea."

"She called me for advice. I wasn't helpful." Molly rubbed her forehead. "Sorry."

"Not your fault. She's been up and down about the whole thing."

"I heard that." Ciara shouted. "Tell her I don't need an aunt to protect me."

"She's really hurt." Molly rubbed at her eyes. "I didn't mean to upset her. Please tell her I'm sorry. I didn't mean to drag my stuff into her life."

Hanna relayed the message and Ciara snorted, then the door slammed.

"Give her time to calm down." Hanna said. "Are you okay?"

"Mostly." Molly dropped her head. "Thanks Hanna. Let me know she's okay."

"I will." Hanna hung up and Molly dropped her phone again.

"Need a hug?" Blue asked.

"Not right now." Molly curled into a ball.

Blue tucked the blanket around her again. "I'm here when you need me."

***

Ciara stomped through the snow, hood up around her head, but the wind still blew around her ears. She wanted to stop the raging flood that overwhelmed her, but she didn't know how. Hands shoved deep in her pockets, Ciara let her feet take her where ever they wanted.

The night grew colder, and snow started to fall. Ciara shivered, maybe she should go home. But then she'd have to talk to Grandma and the last thing she wanted to do was talk to an adult. A shape moved on the road in front of her and Ciara gasped and fell to her knees. She couldn't think, her heart beat so fast it hurt, tears flowed down her face in icy trails.

"Hey, you okay?" A girl a few years older than Ciara stared down at her with a frown.

"You're Dean's sister." Ciara blurted, then covered her face. *I'm such a dufus.*

"Dean is my brother." The girl reached down and offered Ciara a hand. She pulled Ciara to her feet with surprising strength.

"I'm Ciara." Ciara rubbed her face with her hands.

"He's mentioned you once or twice." The girl grinned. "A minute that is. I'm Sophie."

"Hullo." Ciara stared at the ground. "Please don't tell Dean about this?"

Sophie laughed and patted Ciara's shoulder, then made a zipping motion over her lips. "Us girls gotta stick together. Better get you home before parts start freezing and falling off."

They walked through the snow. Strangely, Ciara's insides warmed up despite the dropping temperature.

At Ciara's home, Sophie slapped Ciara's back. "Next time you storm out of the house, make sure you have mitts and a hat. Don't be a stranger."

Ciara hung up her coat and put her boots on the mat, then slowly walked into the kitchen. "I'm sorry, Grandma. I didn't mean to get so nasty."

"We'll chalk it up to a lesson learned."

"So I'm not grounded?" Ciara asked.

"Do you want to be?"

"No." Ciara hugged her Grandma. "Thanks for being my Grandma."

"I'm glad you're feeling better."

***

He walked through the dark, stoking the heat of his anger. The city was full of disgusting people. Addicts, crazy people, criminals. It wasn't his fault; those people were weak. If they had been good, they wouldn't have died. A shape huddled in the trees. Another one, he'd clean up the city by himself if he had to. His heart raced and he picked up a rock.

# CHAPTER 11
**Thursday November 25**

Ferguson stared at the crime scene. A man in a sleeping bag had been beaten with a rock. He probably never woke to know what was going on. The killer had made no attempt to disguise their actions. Blood spattered the ground. They had left a footprint in the blood, but unless the shoe was a very rare make, it wouldn't likely be much help. The scene of crime people were busy processing the area

"Why kill a homeless person?" Hassim shook her head. "Especially in their sleep?"

"There's been a backlash since Bajwa's murder on Friday." Ferguson grated his teeth. "Callister got between some self-appointed street cleaners and their victim on Monday."

"I saw the news clip." Hassim scanned the organized chaos around them. "I sort of hoped that would be the end of it."

"No such luck. It isn't on the news, but the social media pages are blowing up with people demanding something be done."

"As long as it isn't in their neighbourhood and they don't have to pay for it." Hassim heaved a sigh. "You think our killer is a vigilante gone too far?"

"Possibly." Ferguson tucked his hands under his arms to warm them. "I'm going to take look around the area, see if anything shows up."

"Good idea." Hassim pointed. "I'll cover the space between here and the bridge."

Ferguson nodded and walked the opposite direction. He didn't know what he was looking for so he prowled along the path looking for anything that looked out of place. He spotted a blank space in the snow where grass showed through. Footprints walked off the path to the spot, then back on the asphalt. To his eyes they looked similar to the print in the blood. He used his phone to snap pictures, then called the SoC people.

"Ferguson here. I think I have a secondary crime scene." He waved as someone looked around for him.

"Okay, someone's heading over now."

A woman civilian team member walked over with yellow caution tape and a black bag. "What's up?"

"I have a hunch the killer picked up the rock here." Ferguson pointed to the blank spot and the prints."

"Gotcha." She took a camera from the bag and number markers and started recording the scene.

"What did you find?" Hassim came up beside him.

"I think the killer picked up the rock here." Ferguson waved at the prints and blank spot.

"I didn't think they carried it with them from home." Hassim said.

"Of course not, but it shows an action on impulse. There's someone sleeping in the bushes, here's a rock, I should bash them on the head."

"Right." Hassim shivered. "I hope they don't make a habit of it."

***

Molly sat in the briefing meeting, pushing the unsteady feelings of the past couple days aside.

"We've been hearing that a lot more of our clients are being harassed." Don scanned the room. "We need to support them without being pulled into altercations."

Did he look at Molly when he said that? She breathed in slowly, out slower. She could do this.

"Molly, a reporter has asked to shadow one of our teams, I'd like you to show her around. Take her to the Loop or the Café. Make sure she sees the kind of work we do."

He handed out the rest of the assignments and Molly left with the rest of the workers. Cheryl turned out to be a woman in her forties, dressed carefully, but warmly. She beamed at Molly.

"I'm working on an article." Cheryl tucked her blond hair under her knit cap. "Maybe if people had a better sense of what it is like to be homeless, they wouldn't go off the handle so quickly."

"Here's hoping." Molly checked her bag and added more granola bars and water. "We'll head down Tranquille to the Loop. That's a good place to start."

"Lead on." Cheryl patted her pockets. "Would it be a problem if I recorded the interviews?"

"I suspect most people will clam up if they're going on tape. You can always ask, but I'd build a rapport with them first. Listen, respond to their concerns. Street people have the same needs for connection as any of us."

"I see." Cheryl made a note in a small book and stuffed it back in her pocket. They walked south, the cold wind blowing around Molly's feet. She would have to thank Ciara for helping her find the new boots. A woman Molly knew as Maggie shivered in a thin coat as she came over to Molly.

"I got a place, but nothing to move into it. I can't live on the floor."

"Check with the office and see if they have any leads. The Loop may also be able to help."

Maggie frowned at Molly. "You'd think someone would have this covered."

"You're right, it is a problem. I'll bring it to my manager and see if he has anything to suggest." Molly handed Maggie a card. "Check in at the office or call in the next few days."

"I don't have a few days."

"Come with me and I'll get someone at the Loop to look into it."

"You can't do anything yourself?" The frown deepened.

"My job is to connect you to resources. I can't fix everything myself."  She smiled at the woman. "It's only a short walk."

"I know where the Loop is." Maggie dropped the card on the sidewalk. "I thought you could help."

Molly watched the woman walk north and sighed.

"Are there many like her?" Cheryl asked. "You'd think she be happy for whatever she got."

"She wants a place to live." Molly said. "Not a room to camp out in. It is hard enough asking for help, getting a suggestion to ask for more help probably doesn't feel good. In another life she could be driving an SUV and asking for the manager at whatever store she is shopping at. People are people, and those on the street are no different, though many struggle with burdens we can only imagine."

"Okay." Cheryl made a note in her book, and they walked the rest of the way to the Loop.

"Victor, keep a watch out for Maggie, she's looking for furniture for her apartment."

"Okay." He closed the door behind them. "I'll put out a few feelers."

"Thanks, Victor." Molly led Cheryl to a table. "Hi Zeke."

Zeke looked up and then returned to holding his coffee with cupped hands.

"I'll get us some coffee." Molly pointed to a chair. "Have a seat and I'll be right back. How do you like your coffee?"

"Cream and a sweetener." Cheryl sat at the table while Molly fetched the coffee. "Have you been to the Loop before?"

"Not really, I did a story on the Covid Meal train a couple years back."

"The Loop is run mostly by volunteers. They have a small core of paid workers, all of whom have lived experience."

"Lived experience?" Cheryl sipped at her coffee.

"People who have been homeless or are recovering addicts. Many of the volunteers started out as guests."

"Guests?" Cheryl raised an eyebrow.

"Everyone who comes in through the door is a guest. They are welcomed, offered food and drink and maybe other things."

"Like furniture for an apartment."

"Or like a need to gain perspective on the life of someone living homeless." Molly smiled. Cheryl took another drink of her coffee.

"Someone bashed in Pat's head last night." Zeke didn't look up from his mug. "Hank fell down a hill and died of the cold. Wendy OD'd. Gonna be a hard winter."

"That's horrible." Cheryl said. "Did you know them well?"

"Saw them around." Zeke hunched over further.

"You have a safe place to stay?" Molly lifted her coffee but didn't drink yet.

Zeke snorted. "There ain't no safe place." He stood and carried his coffee to another table.

Cheryl stared at him.

"Not everyone wants to chat." Molly shrugged. "Being homeless is like living in a fish tank. You don't get to escape the view of others."

"No need to be rude." Cheryl frowned.

"Imagine some random person coming into your kitchen and starting to talk to you."

"But you deliberately sat at Zeke's table."

"Right, and didn't force my attention on him, but allowed him to have his space." Molly put her mug down. "Wasn't so long ago he wouldn't even sit down here. He's beginning to trust the people at the Loop."

Cheryl stared into her coffee and swirled it around. "I thought they'd be friendlier."

"Why?" Molly drank half her cup. "Because they need stuff?"

"Hello, Molly." A woman came up to the table. "We have a bit of breakfast left, you want any?"

"Sure, Barbara." Molly gestured to Cheryl. "Cheryl is working on a story about life on the street."

"What do you want to know?" Barbara sat in Zeke's empty chair and leaned forward to talk to

Cheryl. Molly sat and listened to them chatter. Cheryl making notes in her book. Molly refilled her cup and returned to the table.

"Oops, better get to work." Barbara jumped up and headed into the kitchen.

"Did she really own a multi-million dollar business?" Cheryl put her notebook away.

"Very possibly." Molly caught Cheryl's eyes. "She does the bookkeeping for the Loop."

"You let her handle the money?"

"It's her job." Molly frowned. "Why is she inherently less trustworthy because you met here instead of a high-end restaurant?"

"But they..." Cheryl waved a hand as if trying to catch the right word.

"There is no they." Molly shifted so she could face Cheryl. "Just us. An alcoholic, a sex worker, those are the images that come to mind when we think homeless, but they're just like you and me, except they aren't lucky enough to have a place to call home. There's also the university student who lives in his car because he can't find an apartment that will allow him to keep his cat, or the woman who leaves an abusive relationship with nothing but the clothes she's wearing."

"I see this article is going to harder to write than I thought." Cheryl smiled as Barbara put plates in front of them.

"Sorry, there wasn't as much left as I thought."

"No worries." Cheryl picked up the fork.

Molly took Cheryl by Spero house, explaining the idea of supportive housing.

"Can we go to a shelter?" Cheryl asked.

"It's a bit of a walk, but sure." Molly called the shelter as they crossed the Overlander to Emerald house. One of the workers met them and gave a quick tour.

"Why sleep on the street if there are shelters?" Cheryl looked up at the green building.

"The shelters are full." Molly walked east toward the Mustard Seed. "Some people don't trust them, or don't like the rules, or they've been banned for some reason. We'd need at least double the capacity to really serve the community, and even then, we wouldn't have shelter for everyone."

"Oh."

By the time Molly brought Cheryl back to the Streetreach office, she was cold and tired, and Cheryl's book was full of scribbles.

"Thanks for the help, Molly." Cheryl smiled as she opened her car door. "Here's my card."

Molly waved goodbye. She went back into the office, there was paperwork to do.

As she walked her phone rang.

"Molly, it's Tad." His voice was hesitant.

Her first instinct was to hang up, but she pushed it away. "Talk then."

"I'd rather talk in person. I miss you."

"I wonder why?" Molly gripped her phone tighter.

"I needed time to think."

"You could have said that." She stopped on the sidewalk. "But you ghosted me, even your phone was disconnected."

"My phone was stolen, and I had to cancel it."

"You all right?"

"They took it out of my car." Tad said. "I'm fine."

"You have a car?" Molly put her hand to her head. "When did that happen?

"I've always had one."

"The first time we went out, you told me the car was your father's."

"Technically it is part of his fleet." Tad's confidence returned. "I didn't want to come across like some rich kid slumming."

"You volunteered to cook at the Loop." Molly couldn't get her thoughts in order.

"I like to cook; it gave me something to do." Tad chuckled. "Not needing to work gets boring."

"Right." Molly fought the urge to smash her phone.

"Let's go out on Tuesday. I'll take you out for a nice meal before the show."

"I will think about it and let you know by Monday." Molly hung up and shoved the phone into her bag. She stalked along Vernon, her boots slamming into the concrete. He'd been lying the whole time. Was the Tad she knew even real? But she'd enjoyed going out with him. Holding hands and hugging was a new experience for her.

What does he really think of me?

Her anger took her home before she realized it. Blue had got home first and put a meal in the oven. She could hear the shower running. As little as she wanted to talk about Tad, she needed to. Molly didn't like the way she felt, like a porcupine had replaced her heart.

The phone rang again, but it was Hanna's number.

"Hi." Molly tried to keep the heat out of her voice.

"Uh, is it good time to talk?" Ciara asked.

"Sorry, I'm just a bit pissed off at the moment." Molly took a deep breath. "Not your fault."

"I'm sorry about last night. I was really bitchy."

"We all have days like that." Molly sat more comfortably. Tad could wait. "It's not like anything you do will make me love you less."

"Thanks Molly." Ciara giggled. "Let me tell you what happened later."

Molly listened to the story shaking her head. "Sounds like you had quite a time. I'm glad you're safe."

"Sophie said hello to me at school. She's so cool. A top student, but still has lots of friends. She introduced me to some of them."

"What did Dean think of that?"

"I'm not sure, every time I looked at him, he turned red."

"Don't wait too long to talk to him." Molly stared at the ceiling. The whole ceiling was white, but it had been painted in different lustres. She'd never noticed that before.

"I know, I'm going to call him tonight. I want to be friends."

"Not boyfriend/girlfriend?"

"Grandma says I'm too young to have a boyfriend." Ciara didn't sound worried about it. "I think I agree with her, for now."

Molly laughed. "That's the Ciara I know."

"What if I get bitchy again?" Ciara whispered. "I tried to stop, but I couldn't."

"Just say you're in a bad mood. Then you can talk it out."

"What if I don't feel like talking?"

"Then you make space for yourself until you do."

"I don't know." Ciara said.

"Practice with small emotions." Molly lay out on the couch. "Don't wait for the big ones to overwhelm you."

"Is that what you do?"

"Still working on it." Molly sighed. "I don't think it's something you perfect. I need to remind myself that my emotions are valid, but I'm more than my feelings."

"I don't get it." Ciara huffed. "I'll work on it. I gotta go now."

"Love you." Molly said and hung up.

***

He wandered through the city carrying an iron prybar. Thoughts of the previous night made him alternately excited and nauseous. What was he doing? It isn't like they didn't deserve it. They were probably better off dead. He wouldn't look for anyone, but if he happened upon one, it would be fate.

The sound of shouting drew his attention. Three men were beating up a homeless person, genderless beneath countless layers of clothing.

"We don't want your kind here." One of the attackers kicked the curled form of their victim on the ground. The other two limited themselves punches. "Get out of town." The speaker gripped his victim's face and glared. "If we find you again it will be worse." With a final boot to the face, the trio left the person lying on the ground.

When he was sure they were gone. He walked up to the person. They lay writhing on the ground, blood covering their face.

"Help me." The person moaned, trying and failing to get up.

"It just isn't your night." It was fate, he was the angel of death. Retribution for how his city had deteriorated. He lifted the prybar and struck. One blow and the junkie stopped moving. Should he hit them again? No leave it up to fate. They would live or die, and it wouldn't be his responsibility.

Snow fell, silent and beautiful as if the world were giving a benediction to his actions.

# CHAPTER 12
## Friday November 26

Blue turned on the news as he made his breakfast.

"—killed in Riverside Park this morning. The yet unidentified woman is the second homeless person to die by violence. Police are not commenting pending investigation."

Blue lost his appetite, but forced himself to eat the food anyway. It would be a long day and he'd need the energy. He left a note for Molly and headed out to the Loop. He needed to talk with Judy before doing anything.

"The streets are getting dangerous for our people." Blue leaned back in the chair.

"What do you suggest we do?" Judy spread her arms. "We can't patrol people through the night."

"I think we need to put pressure on the city to open more shelter beds." Blue rubbed his head.

"I don't know, Blue. The city will just tell us there is no money."

"Then we do something, an emergency shelter."

"I will run the idea past the board." Judy sighed. "But I can't promise anything. In the meantime, we can suggest that people overnight in groups."

"That's a start." Blue stood. "But I don't think it will be enough. We need the people off the streets."

"I agree." Judy nodded. "But then that is our mission regardless of killers. I'll talk to the board and get back to you."

"Thanks."

Blue caught the number 1 bus getting off on Seymour and walking to the Café. He didn't have a good feeling, but that could be his PTSD. Hopefully that would be it, but he hadn't convinced himself by the time he walked into the Café.

Tad was in the kitchen prepping for lunch.

"You okay, Tad?" Blue studied the younger man. "I don't think you've ever missed a shift without notice before."

"Just some stuff came up I needed to deal with." Tad brushed it off. "I've talked to Molly, so everything is cool."

"I see." Blue turned to leave. "I'll let you get back to work."

He grabbed a cup of coffee and sat down at his desk, but couldn't concentrate on the reports. He'd need the statistics for the end of the month soon. After his coffee, he'd get to work, concentration or not.

***

Molly read Blue's note and a shiver ran through her. Another death. She had trouble getting her head around it. Her clients were the most vulnerable people in the city. They didn't have anywhere to hide if someone was hunting them.

Maybe Don would know more. She ate breakfast quickly and left for work early. The weather wasn't bad for November, but the cold bit into her.

At Streetreach, she knocked on Don's door.

"Come in." He pushed the paperwork aside. "How may I help?"

"Another person died last night."

"And you want to know what we can do about it?"

Molly nodded.

"There isn't much." Don leaned on the desk.

"We can warn our clients to be on the lookout." Molly twisted her hands.

"They probably know as much or more as we do." Don stood and came around the desk. "It is important that you keep work at work, otherwise it will eat up your life."

"I try." Molly looked down.

"It is easier said than done. I know. Let's grab a coffee and get ready for the meeting."

"Okay." She followed him out and made herself a tea, thinking of Hanna. Maybe it would warm her more than coffee.

"You may or may not have heard," Don opened the briefing, "there was another death last night. The police are treating it as suspicious. Keep your ears open while you're on the street. I'm sending you out in pairs as a precaution. People who are scared or angry may act irrationally."

He assigned the areas for the workers and sent them off. Molly was paired up with Beth, a woman who'd graduated a few years back. She had her blonde hair in a ponytail, and wore a sensible coat and boots.

"Let's head down to the River Trail. I saw you'd talked to a few people there earlier this week."

"Sounds good." Molly pulled her hat over her ears and follow Beth out to the street.

"How have you been enjoying the work?" Beth asked.

"Mostly it is good." Molly sighed. "But I wish I could do more."

"I know. We're trying to empty the river with a teaspoon. Sure, our job is to help where we can, but a lot of the time it comes down to just letting people know someone cares enough to see them."

"Caring is important." Molly nodded. "I wouldn't be here if people hadn't cared about me."

"My upbringing wasn't a rough a deal as you had." Beth glanced over at her. "I had a decent family but wanted to impress the wrong crowd. Was scary looking back at it, but I survived and wanted to offer a hand up to other people."

"How do you know about my background?" Molly hunched her shoulders.

"Mostly the news reports. I was an Agatha supporter. You were like a hero to me."

"I didn't feel like a hero." Molly put her hands in her pockets. "I was just trying to survive."

"Aren't we all?" Beth waved a hand. "But you tried to bring people along on the journey with you."

"Never thought of it much." Molly's fists clenched and she told them to relax. "Can we talk about something else?"

"Sorry," Beth shook her head. "I get carried away."

"It's no problem." Molly nodded to a client across the street. "Maybe we should see if she wants to chat."

They spent the day talking with people. All the clients were very aware of the recent deaths, but no one talked about it.

"Not like we can do anything about it." The woman stared at Molly as if challenging her to argue. "It's fate. If I die, I die." She stomped back down to her camp. "Jack, we're done talking."

"Sorry, I gotta go." Jack winced and bounded down to the camp.

"They're an odd couple but have been together for a few years." Beth walked on toward the next camp. "It is easier having someone to watch your back."

***

Ferguson stared at the reports on his desk. The victim was a middle-aged woman. She'd taken quite a beating. What was left of the footprints at the scene suggested more than one attacker. Likely three from the photos they had of prints. Their track weaved on its way to the sidewalk. Probably drunks out to save the world. He shook his head in disgust. His job would be so much easier if people left the world alone.

This attack was different from the bashed head with a rock. That was probably, as Hassim suggested, an impulsive action. Here a victim was deliberately sought out and assaulted by multiple people. Last thing he needed was a wave of vigilantes trying to force the homeless out of town. More people would get hurt and evidence muddied. It became very difficult to connect one person with one crime beyond a reasonable doubt.

Hassim came over to his desk and put a coffee by his hand.

"The snow last night made things difficult." Hassim pulled over a chair. "The lack of disturbance on the sidewalk suggests the attack took place before the snow began to fall. It started at eleven fifteen."

"Mmm." Ferguson took a drink from his coffee. "That's early for the drunks getting out of the bars. They must have found their courage at home."

"It may have been deliberate, the timing I mean." Hassim sipped at her cup. "Anyone with a cell phone could know that snow was expected around that time."

"They went out earlier in the night, so the snow would cover their tracks?" Ferguson played with a pen on his desk. "That is more than the boys getting drunk and going out to lay a beating on someone. It was planned. They went hunting."

"There were no belongings at the scene." Hassim stared into her cup. "I've asked for a wider search of the area, see if anything turns up."

"Good thinking."

"You make a connection to the one before last's attack?" Hassim frowned.

"I haven't seen anything to suggest it."

"Great, so we have an impulsive killer and a bunch who plan their actions." Hassim drained her cup and put it on the desk.

"Actually, that's good news." Ferguson dropped the pen. "It makes it less likely that any more people will die."

"How do you figure?"

Ferguson looked at the pen on the floor and drank his coffee instead of picking it up. "The impulse killer is probably freaked out at what they did and will be lying low. I don't think the beating was meant to be fatal, so the hunters will cool it too."

"Probably took it too far because of the alcohol." Hassim nodded. "I'm good with that.

"Let's start by bringing in the guy Constable Post arrested last week. Maybe the court-date didn't dull his anger." Ferguson picked up his phone and called dispatch, while he brought up the record on his computer. "There's a suspect I'd like picked up. Name's David O'Brian, six three, about two hundred pounds. Has dark hair and blue eyes. I'll send the file to you to pass on the photo." He hung up and forwarded the file. Maybe they'd get lucky and find the guy.

***

"A few of us are going for drinks after work." Beth looked up from the desk. "Why don't you join us?"

"I don't drink." Molly sighed. She would love to make some new friends.

"Coffee's a drink, so's water." Beth grinned at her. "You won't be the only non-alcohol person there. I'm not a drinker either, gave it up when I started to act like a human being again."

"I'll text Blue." Molly pulled out her phone and sent him a quick message.

"Your partner?"

"Adopted father." Molly smiled. "Long story."

"I'd love to hear it; I've heard everyone else's stories more than I need to."

"It isn't that interesting, but I can tell you the high points."

Beth laughed and they returned to their reports.

Molly joined her outside, she recognized the others, but Beth introduced her anyway and they gave their names. Ben, Sari who had lovely long dark hair and Asian features, Karen with bright pink hair and mischievous grin, Andrew had dreads and a bright smile. Molly ran through their names as they walked to Bright Eyes.

She'd never had time, no to be honest, she'd never made time to get to know her co-workers. Inside the bar it was bright and open with huge windows looking out onto the street. They sat down and a server came over and took their orders.

"Ok," Karen pointed at Molly. "We get to hear a new story."

Molly took a deep breath and began her story where Blue interrupted a gang member giving Molly a beating. She didn't go into huge detail about the events, rather she focused on learning to trust, then love Blue, a completely new experience for her at the time. Molly's iced tea had been refilled twice by the time she finished.

"Holy smokes," Karen took a long drink of her beer. "That could be an action movie. You live with Blue and Sam now?"

"No, the apartment caught on fire while I was in Alberta for school. Sam moved to Toronto to be with his son."

"You're kidding, after all that and there's a fire?" Andrew shook his head. "That's crazy."

"I haven't heard any of your stories yet." Molly sipped at her iced tea. "I will be right back." She found the washroom and stared in the mirror as she washed her hands.

"You okay?" Beth came in. "Looked like it was a tough story to tell."

"It can be." Molly nodded at Beth. "Sometimes I wake up and expect to see that drug addict in the mirror.

"I know the feeling." Beth said.

Back at the table Andrew had been appointed to tell a story next. He talked about arriving in Canada from West Congo and learning how to fit into his new home. Molly was fascinated by his desire to be Canadian, but still hold onto his culture.

"Well, it's that time." Karen finished her beer and asked for the bill. "I'll see you on Monday." The others paid their tabs and said their goodbyes.

Ben walked with Molly up to Vernon St.

"It's hard to imagine being as brave as you." He dodged a woman with a big stroller.

"I was in survival mode." Molly held out her hand with a clenched fist. "The really scary part for me was learning to trust. I still struggle with that." She relaxed her hand.

"As long as you're struggling, you're growing." Ben shrugged. "I keep telling myself that."

"Believe it." Molly waved. "Good night, see you Monday."

She arrived home and waved at Blue.

"Looks like you had a good time." He set the table and fetched dinner out of the oven.

"I did." Molly poured water, then sat down while Blue served himself. "I think I'll make a habit of it. It would be helpful to know the team better."

"It is." Blue tucked into his meal.

"Do you have any friends?" Molly played with her fork.

"Not the kind to go out with after work, but I have a good team at the Café, and keep in touch with the folks from the Peer program."

"Okay." Molly speared a piece of sausage. "As long as you're not lonely."

"I'm not lonely." Blue smiled at her.

"Tad called." Molly closed her eyes. *Why was she talking about him?*

"I saw him Thursday and he said he'd talked to you and worked things out."

Molly deliberately ate a bite of the casserole and chewed it carefully.

"We didn't exactly work things out. I told him I'd let him know on Monday if I wanted to continue our relationship in any way."

"I see." Blue frowned. "I wonder if he's overcompensating for a lack of confidence."

"I'd say he seemed over-confident if anything." Molly ate another bite without tasting it. "Talked like it was no big deal getting back together." Her grip on the fork tightened.

"He told me he missed his shift because some stuff came up."

"Yeah, apparently his phone was stolen from his car, so he got a new one with a different number."

Blue's frown deepened. "I'll have to keep an eye on him."

"What if he cuts out again if I say no?"

"Not your problem. You do what you must. There are other people who can cook." He started eating again, and Molly followed his example.

She needed to talk things out with someone, she didn't want to bother Blue. Maybe Ciara and Hanna could be sounding boards. Her phone rang, it was Ciara. "I'm just eating supper, I'll call you back in a bit."

"Okay."

Molly finished up dinner, then put the leftovers away and washed the dishes. It gave her time to put together what she wanted to say. She felt foolish asking a thirteen year old for relationship advice. But it could help strengthen the bond between them.

"Hi, Molly." Hanna answered. "How was your week?"

"More interesting than I like." Molly filled Hanna in about the events of the week.

"I saw the news. You stay safe."

"I don't plan on walking through the city late at night."

"If you have to go somewhere at night, call me or take a taxi."

"I'll be fine." Molly's jaw tightened.

"Please, promise me."

"I promise." Molly said. "I don't want you worrying about me. How's Ciara?"

"Trying very hard." Hannah chuckled. "She came home yesterday with a whole gang of kids. They sat at the kitchen table and did homework. I've never heard anyone have so much fun with schoolwork."

"Was Dean there?"

"He was, and he didn't get any special treatment. I think the idea of a girlfriend or boyfriend is less scary than actually having one."

"Ciara did say something about staying friends." Molly said. "Good for her."

"I'll call her." Hannah called for Ciara. "Molly's on the phone."

"Hi Molly." Ciara said. "Dean and I had a good talk. We're going to be good friends. When we're sixteen we'll decide if we want to go out."

"Smart idea."

"I think Sophie suggested it to him. She knows a lot about that kind of stuff."

"What would Sophie say if she found out a friend had been, not quite lying, but hiding the truth for a long time." Molly's stomach twisted.

"Hmmm, I think it would depend on what the truth was and why they were hiding it."

"He was hiding that he's rich and owns a car and everything."

"Tad's rich?" Ciara squeaked.

"Apparently." Molly sat on the couch and got comfortable. "All along I thought he was someone like me."

"Did you ever ask him?" Ciara said. "I mean maybe he was afraid you'd treat him different if you knew he was rich."

"Didn't think of that." Molly stared into space. "I think it would have been different. I would have been afraid he was trying to buy me."

"Maybe that's the problem. Like, if he'd said, 'oh by the way, I'm rich.' You'd want to step back and think about things."

"How'd you get so smart?" Molly asked.

"I'm just imagining what Sophie would say. She's big on being upfront, but also on second chances."

"You've talked a lot with her."

"I wanted to make sure I didn't mess things up with Dean. She was the one who convinced him to talk to me."

"I'd like to meet this girl." Molly's stomach relaxed. "She sounds like she'd make a great sister-in-law."

Ciara laughed. "I think what you told me helps. I'm not feeling like I'm going to explode all the time."

"I'm glad. Living as a bomb can't be fun."

"Right." Ciara drawled. "Why don't you come visit tomorrow? I'll ask Sophie to drop by and meet you."

"Why not invite Dean too?"

"I don't think he'd be comfortable being the only guy, and this is his older sister after all. I'll ask and let him decide."

"After lunch good?"

"I'll call Dean right away. Bye." Ciara hung up. Molly stretched and saw Blue looking at her with a bemused smile.

"I take it you weren't worried about me hearing your call, or you would have taken it into your room."

"I feel weird going to my room to talk to someone. Don't want you to think I don't trust you."

"Everybody needs privacy now and again." Blue brought the guide up on the TV. "I don't mind."

"Thanks." Molly swivelled to face the TV. "Your turn to choose a movie."

The movie Blue chose ended up being about tracking down a serial killer. Molly huddled under the blanket and watch wide eyed. Not that the movie was gory, but the tension it created was almost unbearable. If she had watched it with Tad, he'd have his arm around her shoulders.

The killer was an ordinary person no one would expect to be so evil. He preyed on street people at first, but then grew bolder and started attacking more affluent victims and stealing their cash. The big break in the case came when he jumped someone who could fight back. The woman ended up on the pavement, bleeding from a knife wound, but the killer fled, limping, into the dark.

She called 911 and gave her description of the man. She made them listen in case she didn't survive.

She did survive at the end of the movie, but it was a close thing. They caught the guy at a hospital getting his injuries treated. No big shoot out, no mind-bending twist to make it work. At the end the guy shrugged and said, 'so you got me,' and allowed himself to be handcuffed and led away.

"That was creepy." Molly shivered.

"More intense than I expected." Blue came over and sat beside her. "Need a hug?"

"Oh yeah," Molly leaned against him. "Thanks"

She went to bed but couldn't sleep. The horror of the ordinary person being so evil kept her awake. *What if the deaths this week were the work of a serial killer?* The thought circled in her head until she dragged herself out of bed and found Sergeant Ferguson's card. Before she could second guess herself, she dialed the number and prayed he wouldn't answer the phone.

"Ferguson here."

"Uh Sergeant Ferguson, this is Molly Callister. Sorry to bother you so late, but I watched this movie, and it creeped me out."

"Right, and you called me why?" Ferguson didn't sound angry.

"What if the first two deaths weren't an accident?" Molly gulped. "What if it is a serial killer?"

Ferguson didn't laugh.

"Must have been some movie. I can't discuss an open case, but we are examining all the possibilities. You can go to sleep."

Molly thanked him and crawled back into bed.

***

Ferguson hung up the phone and scanned the crime scene. The victim lay sprawled on his back, the side of his head caved in. The man's dog, a tiny terrier mix, had survived with a broken leg. A constable had taken it to an emergency vet. The image of Callister's old dog came into his head. If the victim had a dog like that, he'd be alive, and the case would be over.

"What was that about?" Hassim came over.

"Concerned citizen worried there was a serial killer loose in Kamloops."

"You're kidding." Hassim stared at him. "You aren't kidding. What did you tell them?"

"That we were investigating all the angles and she could go to sleep."

"You think that might have been our killer looking for attention?"

"I don't think so." Ferguson rolled his eyes. "It was our old friend Molly Callister. It seemed that she watched a movie that upset her."

"Interesting." Hassim rubbed her hands together. "I kind of liked her after we got past the idea she was a cold blooded killer."

"Don't remind me." Ferguson turned to watch the scene of crime team at work. They marked everything and photographed from several angles. Unfortunately, there wasn't much to photograph, the snow was so disturbed it was impossible to get an idea of the tread. "Last night, what if there were two attackers? One beat up the victim, but left her alive, the second came in and delivered the final blow?"

"It's possible." Hassim adjusted her toque. "It would explain the shift in MO."

"Have we got an MO for the killer yet?"

"They are using some kind of heavy bar, and they are only hitting the victims once. Remember the autopsy report? Last night's vic died of one hard blow to the head with something like a crowbar or the like." Hassim pointed at the crushed skull of the corpse. "That looks like one blow."

"Great." Ferguson huffed. "If their MO is solidifying, they won't stop killing."

"Not until we stop them." Hassim said. "We have to hope they get careless sooner rather than later."

"No kidding." Ferguson had a bad feeling about the case. "I think I'm going to have a talk with Callister. I'm curious about that movie."

# CHAPTER 13
## Saturday November 27

The ringing of Molly's phone woke her.

"Good morning." She sat up and ran fingers through her hair.

"I guess I called a bit early."

"It's okay Sergeant Ferguson, I deserve it after calling you at whatever time of night it was."

"No worries, I was at a crime scene." Ferguson's tone sent a shudder down Molly's back.

"Another death of a homeless person?" Molly didn't want to know the answer.

"I can't discuss that with you." Ferguson said. "It's an open investigation."

"Understood." Molly checked the time, seven am. "Are you phoning me on the way to bed?"

"Got it in one." Ferguson chuckled. "I'm calling about that movie you say gave you nightmares. I'd like to know the title."

"Hold on, I'll check our history on the TV." She walked to the living room and turned the TV on. It only took a few seconds to pull up the show from last night. "It's called 'Ordinary Evil'. It's on pay per view."

"I'll look it up." Ferguson said. "Thanks."

"Glad to help." Molly hung up and went back to bed. Why would Ferguson call about a movie? Maybe he wanted to make sure it was real. If they were looking at a serial killer, her phone call to the crime scene would be problematic. Last thing she wanted was to be a suspect for murder again.

She rolled on her back. All the deaths occurred at night, so someone was stalking the city at night looking for people to kill. Killing at night made sense, there weren't many people around, but after a few days of late nights she'd be exhausted. Maybe the killer didn't have a job. Someone on the verge of homeless might hate the homeless enough to kill, but that was a stretch. Perhaps something a homeless person did had hurt them? *I'm glad I don't do this for a living.*

Molly turned on her side and closed her eyes, maybe she could get more sleep before she had to get up.

***

Molly knocked on Hanna's door. Ciara flung the door opened and dragged her in.

"Sophie's here."

"Okay, good." Molly hung up her coat and removed her boots and put on the slippers she kept at Hanna's

Ciara bounced on her toes. "Dean said he didn't want to come to hang out with his sister, he can do that at home. Maybe it means he'd like to come hang out with me."

"Maybe." Molly laughed. "I heard you had a crowd over doing homework."

"Yeah, we had math and stuff. It was a blast."

They walked into the kitchen. Molly studied the girl sitting at the table, cup of tea in front of her and looking completely comfortable meeting Ciara's aunt. Sophie made jeans and t-shirt look classy. She could easily add model to her list of accomplishments.

"You must be Sophie." Molly extended a hand. "I'm Molly."

"Nice to meet you." Sophie's grip was firm and warm. "Ciara told me so much about her aunt Molly, that I'd be more comfortable calling you auntie Molly."

"I'd be honoured." Molly sat down and Ciara put a cup of tea in front of her and poured one for herself.

"I baked some cookies." Ciara set a plate on the table. "You've been warned."

Sophie laughed and picked up a cookie and took a bite. "Don't think you have a future as a cookie magnate, but these aren't too shabby."

Molly helped herself and had to agree with Sophie.

"So have you talked with Tad?" Ciara grabbed a cookie and ate it in two bites.

"Not since last time." Molly sipped at her tea. "Our talk helped me look at things from a different angle." She summarized the situation and the phone discussion for Sophie, though most likely Ciara had already passed on the details.

"Did he give you any gifts?" Sophie blew on her tea before taking a sip.

"No, we usually took turns paying for the movie and the coffee after. I liked the feeling that I wasn't going in debt to him." Molly gazed at Sophie through the steam from her mug.

"Right, beware of a boy, or a man bearing gifts." Sophie grimaced. "My first boyfriend was always giving me stuff. Little things, a pencil, or chocolates. Then he started assuming he had the right to certain things. Mom suggested I sent him packing. He was furious at the waste of his money. I've stuck with a crowd since then, I wasn't eager to deal with that again."

"No, I can imagine." Molly sipped her tea, giving her time to process this girl who in many ways had a better handle on life than Molly did.

"Dean doesn't do that." Ciara said.

"Dean is broke." Sophie glanced at Ciara. "But you need to pay attention to the relationship. What are you looking for, what is he looking for?"

"I don't know." Ciara hung her head. "I haven't thought about it."

"Don't worry about it for now." Sophie patted Ciara's hand. "You have time to think about it."

"I guess." Ciara brightened and took another cookie from the plate.

"What about someone who is all about protecting you?" Molly cupped her mug and let the warmth give her courage.

"I've heard girls talking about that." Sophie shook her head. "Mostly from other boys. It feels like another kind of ownership."

"I wouldn't know if is about other men, I don't really know any." Molly face heated. "When a guy was trying to pick a fight, he was ready to take it on, but stopped when I asked him."

"What makes you think he's in to be your knight in shining armour?" Sophie tilted her head.

"I was in a video confronting a bully on the street. He called and the first thing he said was he should have been there to protect me. Not was I all right or anything like that. I told him I wanted a friend, not a bodyguard, and he hung up and ghosted me for a week."

"Ouch." Sophie winced. "Maybe he thought you should have said lover, not friend."

"Possibly." Molly stared into her tea. "When I was your age, I was being sold on the street for sex. I have a few hang ups around the subject. We went out for a year every Tuesday and never kissed."

"Did he bug you about it?"

"Not after the first few months."

"Not so bad." Sophie hand her mug to Ciara and mimed pouring into it. She leaned close when Ciara left the table. "Should you really be talking about this stuff in front of Ciara?"

"She knows." Molly looked over at Ciara. "We're handling it."

"You finished talking about me?" Ciara put the mug in front of Sophie and sat down.

"Yep." Molly said. "She was worried my story would be hard on you."

"It is." Ciara picked up a cookie and broke it into pieces. "Sometimes I think it would be easier if I didn't know, but you've always been like that from the time we first met. Sometimes I think if only mom hadn't OD'd she might be a lot like you." She wiped a tear from her cheek.

"If you need to talk." Sophie got up and hugged Ciara. "You know you can call me."

Molly wanted to reach out to comfort Ciara, but something stopped her. Guilt? Shame? Molly's stomach churned.

Then Ciara reached out to Molly. "You always tell me that nothing I do can stop you loving me. It always makes me feel safe. There isn't anything about your past that will make me stop loving you."

Molly clutched Ciara's hand and burst into tears. Her face burned, but somehow, she didn't care.

"The way Ciara talks about you makes you sound like a superhero." Sophie returned to her chair. "I can understand why."

"Superhero?" Molly looked and Ciara handed her a napkin. Molly wiped her face and took a deep breath.

"Drugs are a problem here, like anywhere else. This guy came to talk to the school about being an addict. He'd been shot, gone to prison, tried to kill himself. He'd survived it all and wanted to tell his story so other people might not go through what he did." Sophie grabbed a napkin and patted her eyes. "One of my best friends gave up drugs after that."

"He's braver than I am." Molly said.

"Is he?" Sophie raised an eyebrow. "I thought you looked familiar. We followed the election in class last year. Ciara showed me the video of you standing up to the bully from this week. Sometimes I don't feel like getting out of bed. Everything feels so hopeless, but then I think of the guy who turned his life around, the woman who answered questions about prostitution with no shame or hesitation."

"Maybe we're all heroes, but don't know it because it is just our life." Ciara took Molly's mug and refilled it. "Sophie is an example for everyone, that working hard and doing well can be fun. She's going to go to university and become famous and I'll be able to say she's my friend."

"So now what?" Molly asked.

"We keep doing what we do." Sophie beamed a smile at her.

"Maybe I should give Tad a chance." Molly stared up at the ceiling. "And see what happens."

***

Ferguson looked through the autopsy reports of the first two deaths. They'd been declared accidental, nothing suspicious about them. But they bothered

Ferguson. He was certain they were dealing with a spree killer, and it would only get worse. What was the trigger?

The only event near the onset of the murders was the murder of Pathi Bajwa, most likely by Dennis Colm.

"We need to go back to the family and dig deeper." He called Hassim. "Have some research for you. I'd like you to look into the Bajwa family. Who are the people Pathi made deals with, what connections do they have? Anything that might give us insight into why this killer started, and why the homeless? I don't think it's just because they're vulnerable"

"On it." Hassim hung up.

"And I'll do the legwork. I think another chat with Callister is a good place to start." He put the reports back in their folders and locked them in his desk He didn't have the luxury of waiting so he pulled up his recent history and called her.

"Molly here." Ferguson could hear voices and laughter in the background. He almost felt guilty for what he was about to do.

"Hello?" She said. "Anyone there?"

"Sorry, Miss Callister, but I need to ask for your help."

"My help?" The background noise cut off.

"Yes, where are you. I will come pick you up."

"Am I being arrested?"

Ferguson sat with his mouth open, he should have expected that reaction.

"No, Molly, you aren't being arrested." Ferguson made his voice soft. "But there is an urgent matter which needs your expertise."

"What expertise?" Molly's voice chilled his ear through the phone.

"Social work, specifically the homeless. Please."

"I'll meet you at the Lansdowne Tim Hortons." She paused a long moment. "In half an hour if I hurry, longer if I miss the bus."

"If you miss the bus call me and I will come get you." Ferguson hung up. He pulled over a pad of paper and started organizing the questions he had. There were a lot. He looked at the time and sighed. Time to get to the Tim Hortons. At least his car was unmarked, and he was in civies.

Ferguson bought a coffee to keep him company while he waited. Molly walked in a few minutes later and he waved her over.

"I guessed you didn't want me talking too much about that call." Molly sat across from him.

"Thanks, I should have said something to that effect."

"I left two very curious girls at the house. I told them it was an emergency, then had to assure them it wasn't anyone they knew. Finally told them it was a work thing."

"Right." Ferguson studied the young woman across from him. She practically buzzed with anxiety, but she was here. "Good call."

"So what is this about? Is it the murders?" Molly leaned forward and lowered her voice.

"It is, but I can't tell you much about it here. We should go back to the station."

"Sergeant Ferguson, I recognize at least four people in here. If get up and walk out with a strange man, they'll come to only one conclusion. I'd rather not have to deal with that."

"How do you want to do it?"

"I take the bus home. I'll buzz you in."

"How long do you need?"

"Probably an hour. I think I just missed the connection." She pulled out her phone and opened an app. "Yup, just left."

Ferguson wanted to start picking her brains right away, but this wasn't the place, and she didn't trust him. Not that he blamed her.

"See you in an hour." He watched her walk out and get on a bus. *I don't think I've ever taken a bus.* No matter, he had some time to fill.

"Hey, bub. How do you know Molly?" A gaunt man leaned over Ferguson.

"If we're going to talk, why not take a seat?" Ferguson waved to the other chair.

The man sat across from Ferguson. "How do you know Molly?" His tone hadn't got any friendlier.

"I need someone with her social skills to help me with a project."

The man peered at him with a frown. "What kind of project."

"I can't say, confidentiality and all that, but I can say she's going to help me understand the homeless better."

"Huh, why not just talk to us?" The man leaned back. "You're a cop."

"That's why I hired Molly." Ferguson sipped at his coffee. "You want a cup?"

"Sure, triple triple."

Ferguson stood in line and bought an extra-large coffee and sat down passing it to the gaunt man.

"You expect me to spill my guts over a coffee?" The man took a cautious sip, like he thought it might be drugged.

"I expect you to enjoy your coffee." Ferguson drank some more. "If I was paying you for information, you'd know up front."

"Call me Dave."

"I'm Ferguson."

Dave sat in silence for so long that Ferguson figured the conversation was over. He drank his coffee and listened to the buzz of conversation around him.

"Time for me to go, maybe I'll see you around." Ferguson stood.

"Catch the devil, copper. The one that's killing us." Dave gazed at Ferguson. "Don't be dragging our Molly into any trouble."

"I'll watch her back." Ferguson left the store. As he drove to Molly's place, he played back the conversation with Dave. *Shouldn't be surprise the street community know what's up.* If he was going to find a witness, it would most likely be one of the homeless. The challenge would be getting them to talk.

***

Molly perched on the couch waiting for Ferguson to buzz her. Blue sat in his chair watching some program on TV. He looked far too relaxed. Ferguson had said he wanted her help, but her years of being on the street screamed 'trouble, run away'.

She tried slow breathing until she got dizzy, but the anxiety wouldn't leave. *I'll have to live with it.* The buzzer made her jump. Molly checked the video, then let Ferguson in. Two minutes later he knocked. She opened the door and waved him in.

"Welcome, Sergeant Ferguson."

"Just call me Ferguson." He took off his coat and boots. Molly hung the coat in the closet. Somehow, he was less threatening in his stocking feet. He carried a black folder into the living room

"Thanks...Ferguson. This is Blue, my father."

"I believe we've met." Ferguson said and winced.

"You saved Molly's life." Blue smiled and waved to the other chair. "Make yourself comfortable."

"What exactly are you looking for from me?" Molly sat on the edge of the couch.

"It is about the murders of the homeless people." Ferguson said and pulled piece of paper from his folder. "This is a non-disclosure agreement. It essentially says you agree not to talk publicly about the case."

"What is the expiration date?" Blue asked.

"Ten years." Ferguson handed the paper to Blue to read.

"I can't say anything about my work?" A pang went through Molly as she thought of the Friday afternoon coffee and conversation. *This would make a great story.*

"Nothing except that you are working as a civilian with the police. I don't expect it to take up so much time you will miss work. I will write a letter to your supervisor to explain things. The temptation will be to talk about the case because you know something others don't." Ferguson frowned slightly and Blue nodded.

"Okay, I can do that." Molly shoved her disappointment away. This was the way it had to be, and she wasn't going to turn away an opportunity to help her clients. "I'd like to be able talk with Blue. He's an important part of my support system."

"I will sign the agreement too," Blue reached over and handed the paper to Molly. "The other exception is someone bound by confidentiality, such as a doctor or a lawyer."

"That's right, you were a cop." Ferguson turned his gaze to Blue.

"Long time ago."

"I will push it past the inspector." Ferguson handed a pen to Molly. She flattened the paper and read it carefully, then looked at Blue. He nodded, so she put the form on the coffee table and signed it. Blue took it back and signed under her signature and handed to it to Ferguson.

"Time is of the essence." Ferguson handed her the folder. "This must not leave your house. It is information that public isn't privy to."

"I will read it immediately." Molly's hands shook as she put the folder on the coffee table in front of her.

"I have a few general questions you may be able to answer." Ferguson took a notebook and pen from his pocket.

"Okay." Molly sat back and took a deep breath. "I will do what I can."

"First if a homeless person witnessed one of the murders, would they be likely to go to the police?"

"Depends." Molly's mind threw out answers for her. "Some people who sleep in their cars because they can't find a place to live, would still have the assumption that cops are useful and can be trusted. People who have been on the street for a long time trust the cops less. They are more likely to have been ticketed for nuisance complaints, or ended up in jail for a few days. Those people see a system that steamrolls them. They barely trust the street social workers, and we've been out working with people for years."

"Pretty much what I thought." Ferguson smiled wryly. "We aren't always popular with the housed people either. Another good reason not to talk too much about this work. You don't want to be seen as collaborating with the cops. Is there any informal structure in the homeless community? People that others look to for advice and help?"

"That's a good question." Molly frowned in thought. "I know a few people who came into the Loop or the Café for the first time, then we had a swell in the number of guests. I doubt they think of themselves as any kind of leader. They just help out and have been at it longer."

Ferguson made a note. "I wondered if there was something like with the gangs."

"Most people are more afraid of the gangs than the cops. Some gang members couch surf at other members' places. They are dangerous because they want to be seen as dangerous, sometimes they'll randomly beat up a street person to gain cred. They know a homeless person is unlikely to say anything about it. The hatred of anyone who is a rat, runs deep in the gangs and the street." Molly's stomach was settling down. This was like answering questions in university.

"Makes sense." Ferguson made another note. "I know how important people's possessions are. Would they usually sleep near their stuff to keep it safe?"

"Unless they have a storage space to keep stuff, leaving anything lying out is asking for trouble."

"The only victim to be near his stuff, was the first definite murder. The others didn't have anything around them."

"If the threat was great enough, I guess they would run and leave their belongings."

"Such as being chased by people who are looking to cause trouble for the homeless."

"Possibly, some have more attachment than others."

"We try to have a worker outside while we're open, so our guests feel safer leaving their carts outside." Blue shrugged his shoulders. "There are a few who won't let their possession out of arms reach. We provide take-out meals for them."

Ferguson nodded at Blue then looked down at his list. "One more and I'll leave you to read the files. In your estimation how likely is the killer to be homeless?"

"It is faintly possible, but the homeless are more often the victims of crime." Molly leaned forward, but Ferguson held up a hand.

"Thank you for your help. I am aware of the reality of crime on the streets, but it suggests we don't need to send constables out to question people."

"Okay. I'll keep my ears open." Molly sat back. "But I won't question our clients for you."

"I wouldn't expect you to. Interrogation is an art." Ferguson stood and put his notebook away. "Your job is to advise us to make our work more effective. Don't under any circumstance act like a police officer."

"Right." Molly nodded vigorously.

Ferguson collected his coat and boots. "When you've read the files call me with any thoughts. I know you have the direct number to my cell."

Molly closed the door behind him. She leaned against the door. "Why me?"

"You appear to have made an impression on him."

"I should never have called him."

"You called him?" Blue arched his brows.

"After that movie." Molly's face grew warm. "I couldn't sleep, so I called Sergeant Ferguson to ask if there was a serial killer attacking street people."

"What was his reaction?"

"I think he was more amused than anything else." Molly lifted her head.

"Did he answer your question?"

"I think he just did." Molly opened the folder and started reading through the files.

***

"What do you have for me?" Ferguson sat at his desk while Hassim relaxed in a chair.

"The Bajwa family has fingers in a lot of pots. Development deals, business investments, and the show piece, the car dealership."

"Why 'show piece'?" Ferguson lifted an eyebrow.

"Most of their dealings are in the background. Nothing shady, but they don't spread the word of their involvement."

"Any indication that his death is going to knock over a house of cards?"

"Pathi was the face of the dealership, but his wife, Rutvi was the brains behind their investments. As far as I can tell they are all money makers. Not much for any single deal, but put them together it adds up to a substantial income."

"Did he have a will registered?"

"Pretty much what you'd expect. Everything to the wife, the kids get enough to keep them happy. Peter inherits his father's share of the dealership."

"Who else has shares?" Ferguson leaned back in his chair.

"Rutvi has one third of the business, Peter had a fifth and inherits his father's third. I haven't tracked down the others. Most of them are numbered corporations."

"What about numbered corporations for the Bajwas?"

"They have a few but compared to some I've seen, theirs are straightforward business companies. It doesn't look like they're hiding anything. Either that they are better at hiding than most."

"Good." Ferguson swung back and forth in the chair. "I looked at the first two autopsy reports. The first was death by exposure, the second by overdose. Not much mystery about that."

"What if they were accidents?" Hassim leaned forward. "The first could have been pushed and fell down the slope."

"The second, the overdose could hardly be an accident. There was no sign of any struggle."

"The needle was in her neck. That's unusual enough to look at. Maybe she fumbled the needle, and the killer snatched it up and injected her."

"That would be impossible to prove." Ferguson stopped swinging and leaned on the desk. "Occam's razor would say an overdose is an overdose."

"I don't say we are going to charge anyone for it." Hassim frowned, "But the timing and escalation make sense. Next is an impulse crime with a handy rock."

"The vic was only struck once. Might have lived if he'd got to the hospital. The last two were single blows as well." Ferguson pulled the reports from his locked drawer. "The killer hits once, then lets fate decide if the person lives or dies. That way they can convince themselves it isn't their fault"

"If he sticks to the pattern, the chance of someone surviving grows."

"True, but the weather is helping them. It's iffy enough sleeping outside, add a severe injury to that and there isn't much hope." Ferguson sat up straight. "Callister agreed to advise on the case. She gets the files but won't be at the crime scene. Photos will have to do."

"I thought you were nuts and she'd turn you down flat."

"She has a lot of passion for helping her people, and those people are the homeless."

"Anything useful yet?"

"She knows her stuff about the street. Everything she said matched up with my experience. She'll passively listen for information about the case from her clients, but she refused to ask questions."

"Good, no need to muddy the water if we need to talk to them." Hassim slapped her knees and stood up. "I'm going home to sleep before we get the call tonight."

"You sure we'll get a call?" Ferguson put the trash in the garbage can and locked up the files.

"Want to make a wager?" Hassim grinned at him.

"Hell no. I'll see you later."

***

He dressed in his night gear as he thought of it. The only thing in his pockets was the car key. The mask, gloves, and bar he put behind the seat. His stomach ached with nausea, but his hands were shaking with eagerness. He was the hand of fate, winnowing the lowest of the low.

The car started without a sound. The electric car wasn't practical most of the time, but it made an excellent vehicle to hunt. There would be lot of activity around the river. He'd try Sahali tonight.

Cruising the dark streets increased his anticipation. He wasn't supposed to care. He was the even, merciless hand of fate. The grip of his fingers on the wheel put the lie to that. The parks here were smaller, riskier. But he'd read about the scourge of the homeless reaching even here. He had a hard time believing it.

He didn't see the person with the cart until the last second. It was full of cans and bottles. His excitement overflowed and he swerved toward the person and punched the accelerator. Still, he hardly more than bumped the person down the steep hill, but the cart flipped, and cans clattered behind him.

It wasn't right. He couldn't be the hand of fate if he didn't follow the rules. He drove home and parked in the garage. There was no damage to the car. He dashed to the bathroom to vomit in the toilet. He'd done it wrong; it was no good. Slumped on the cold floor he promised himself that he would do better tomorrow.

# CHAPTER 14
## Sunday November 28

Molly had nightmares all night from reading the files. Even with the worst of them redacted, they were disturbing. Add in that she'd found one of the bodies and knew another one to talk to and she had to fight the urge to curl into a ball and withdraw completely from the world.

But she had a job to do, and she'd known it wouldn't be easy. There were people counting on her, and others who could be pulled into the violence.

Molly soaked in the shower until she'd returned half-way to normal, then got up and made tea. She pulled up her computer and did a search on spree killers. There wasn't much and it didn't do much good to point her in any useful direction. The narcissism made her think of so many different people that again it wasn't much of a help.

Next, she went over the victims to find any commonality aside from that they were all homeless. The only thing she came up with was the victims were marginal even for the street community. None of the victims had visited the Loop or the Café as far as she could see. She'd get Blue to check when he got up. The man with the dog had used the dog's reputation for being vicious to avoid social interaction with anyone but a small circle. None of them were people known to accept help willingly. She didn't know about the sleeping man and the woman in the park as they hadn't been identified yet.

It suggested they needed to work harder on reaching and warning the fringes. But likely they wouldn't listen anyway. She'd talk to Don about that. Maybe spread the word to avoid dark deserted places? They'd have to get bylaws to relax enforcement on the more visible safe places to sleep. They were already working on getting more winter beds. The more people who went to a shelter, the more available the less remote night spots became.

How to get possible witnesses to contact the police? There was a huge chasm of distrust there. Most would hesitate to report a crime for fear of the system pulling them in. There was the Crimestoppers tip line, but that assumed access to a phone. Confidential as it might be, it was also a bit of a process. Would people be willing to go through the trouble?

Her phone rang.

"Molly here."

"Good morning any thoughts for us?" Ferguson sounded far too cheery for this early in the morning.

"What makes you so happy?" Molly made coffee while she talked on the phone.

"The killer didn't strike last night."

"Any other deaths?" Molly held her breath.

"A hit and run in Sahali. A man who'd been collecting cans and bottles for a drive was hit and knocked down a steep slope. The initial impact wouldn't have killed him, but he rolled badly and smashed his head against a rock."

"Like Hank, the first death." Molly's heart sank. "Was he pushing a cart holding the cans and bottles?"

"Yeah, he was." Ferguson said. "The cans and stuff were scattered all over the road."

"Late at night?"

"About nine pm, but plenty dark. That's earlier than the other cases as far as we know."

"Still he might have looked like a homeless person pushing a cart if the street wasn't well lit. It's reasonable that the killer would have a car. No buses run at night, and it's pretty cold to be out walking between eleven and dawn. Have you looked at the traffic cams to see if someone walked across the bridge on any of the nights in question?"

"We have someone running through the tapes for the nights in question, but nothing useful yet." Ferguson sounded annoyed.

"I know you've probably thought about all these things already. But I have to check."

"True." Ferguson said. "It would overload to you give you the complete picture of what is being done. Try to stick to the question of the victims."

"Sorry." Molly sighed. "The only thing I have so far is the victims have all been on the margin even for street people. They weren't people to ask for help."

"Interesting, so they would be more vulnerable than the average homeless person?"

"I'm thinking so." Molly paused as a thought struck her. "How is the killer finding their victims? Driving around would be mostly unproductive and anyone they spotted would be reasonably well lit. The killer has to have some way of narrowing the search. Hold on." Molly typed on her computer and scanned the results.

"What do you have?" Ferguson asked.

"How does the general public learn about homeless people? Through the media. I'm scanning through recent articles about the homelessness problem and trying to see if there is a pattern of what parts of the city get mentioned most."

"Let me know what you find." Ferguson hung up and Molly crawled further down the rabbit hole. Her search not only brought up the news sources, but postings to particular groups on facebook. One group had a map they claimed to update daily with where homeless people had been spotted. The downtown was thick with sightings. Both shores of the Thompson and the west side of the North Thompson along Schubert also had heavy concentrations of sightings. Columbia Street and Sahali were more active than she'd expected. Silly, since she knew they had an outreach van in the area. They wouldn't do that for a minimal population. All the certain victims of the killer had died within a few tens of meters from the water. They were places with easy access by car.

Molly sent an email to Ferguson with a screenshot of the map and the link to the group. 'How much police activity was happening near the river? Could that have pushed the killer up to Sahali as a second-choice location?' She sighed and fetched a coffee as a distraction from chill working on the case gave her.

***

Ferguson hung up the phone and took a deep breath. He'd brought her in, he needed to have more patience, but most of what she'd been thinking duplicated lines of inquiry he'd already set in motion. Knowing the victims were on the fringes of the fringe of Kamloops community didn't open any doors either.

Her theory about the hit and run annoyed him since he'd not thought of it, and it was faintly possible. He phoned dispatch to find out who had worked the scene.

"Ferguson here."

"What can I do for you?" The woman on the other end sounded as harried and annoyed as he felt.

"I'll make this quick. What are the chances the hit and run was a deliberate attack?"

"Pretty much a hundred percent. The driver swerved onto the sidewalk and from the distance the victim was thrown, had to have been doing a lot more than the speed limit here."

"What was the victim wearing?"

"Jeans and an old parka, we haven't found a hat, but his wife says he wore a ball cap when he went out."

"Shit." Ferguson smacked his head. "Do me a favour and shoot me everything you have on the case as soon as you have it. Email is Ferguson at blah blah blah."

"Got it." The woman sounded a bit more energized. "I'll have a draft to you by the end of the day."

"Thanks." Ferguson hung up, then dialed Hassim.

"Hassim here. I thought I was going to get to sleep in. What's up?"

"We didn't get called out for a crime scene, but there is a possibility the killer struck anyway. How fast can you get here?"

"I've already left." Hassim hung up.

The chime for the email sounded just as Hassim walked in.

"You look pissed off, what's got your goat?"

"Callister had a brain wave, and it looks possible it will pan out."

"Oh?" Hassim leaned over his shoulder. "What's that email about? It's from Callister."

Ferguson opened the email and read it quickly.

"Crap, she may be onto something." Hassim said.

"It does answer the question of how the killer has consistently found victims. Go through the list of members and see if any have connection to the case."

"What are the odds?" Hassim clicked on the link and looked the number of members. "There's almost three thousand members. It will take me a while."

"Okay, let me know." Ferguson had a thought and glanced at the clock. Only eight o'clock, he'd have to wait a while. He checked the rest of his emails and messages. No sighting of O'Brian. He looked closer at the file on the man and found an address.

"There's a familiar name." Hassim said.

"That was quick."

"Remember David O'Brian? He's an administrator for the group." Hassim grinned at Ferguson. "You want to go and ruin his day?"

"Sounds like a plan." Ferguson took a file from his drawer. "I pulled the file on him when we asked for him to be picked up. Give me a minute to refresh my memory."

***

Hassim parked the car in the driveway of a house on Yew St. Ferguson climbed out and walked around the cars parked in front of the house. Neither the truck nor the SUV showed any damage sustained from a hit and run.

"What are you doing?" The front door opened, and a belligerent man shouted at them. He wore sleep pants and a t-shirt and slippers on his feet.

"He fits the description." Hassim said. "But he looked happier in his mug shot."

"I'm not joking around." O'Brian hefted an aluminum bat. "Leave or I make you. He spat toward Hassim. "I don't want your kind around."

"You mean police officers?" Hassim held up her I.D. and Ferguson followed suit. She pushed the adrenaline away. She didn't need it here. At least not yet.

"Bring them here, I want a close look at them." O'Brian let the end of the bat drop to the front step.

"The bat disappears." Hassim replaced the ID and pulled out a pair of handcuffs. "Or we arrest you and take you to the station."

"For what?" O'Brian sneered.

"Uttering threats to a police officer." Hassim swung the cuffs. "We talk here or at the station, or we talk here on your porch. All depends on what you do in the next five seconds."

"I know my rights." O'Brian hoisted the bat again. "You have to show me the ID close up."

"Five." Hassim held up a hand with all fingers spread. She didn't want it anyway near her taser. Was she reacting to the asshole or to the situation?

"I have a right to defend my property."

"Four." Hassim tucked the thumb away. She didn't like the guy, but that had nothing to do with her job.

A woman in jeans and a housecoat stepped through the door and snatched the bat away from him, returned to the house, and closed the door. Hassim was sure she heard the lock click. She grinned.

"Three."

O'Brian wilted. "You're violating my rights. I can protect my home."

"Not like this you don't." Hassim tucked away the handcuffs. "You are allowed to use reasonable force against an attacker. We aren't attacking, we're standing her talking politely."

"You going to arrest me?" He stuck his chin out as if daring her.

"No, we'll talk out here."

O'Brian banged on the door. "Bring my damned coat out here." When he got no answer, he banged harder and screamed through the door. "Bring my coat woman or I'll beat you within in an inch of your life."

Hassim made a move to step forward, but the door flung open, and the woman stood glaring at O'Brian.

"Are you really that stupid?" She crossed her arms on her chest. "I've had enough of you and your threats. Get out and don't come back. One of your no-good friends can come pick up your shit."

Ferguson stepped up to O'Brian and snapped cuffs on him, but O'Brian didn't react. He stared at the woman and tears started rolling down his cheek.

"You can't do that. This is my home."

"No it ain't. You just lived here, now you don't. That's why I made you sign that paper before you moved in." She looked at Hassim. "Don't bring him back."

Hassim walked over and handed the woman a card. "Call for help if you need it. There are a lot of resources to help you."

"I have a drawer full of these cards." The woman tucked the card in a pocket of her housecoat. "This time I'm gonna listen." She shut the door and the lock clicked, then the rattle of a chain going being set in place.

"Come with me." Ferguson tugged on O'Brian's arm and led him to the car and put him in the back seat. Hassim got into the driver's seat and started up the car while Ferguson walked around to get into his seat.

Hassim drove to Battle St. station with the only sound being the non-stop swearing from the back seat. Ferguson picked up the radio. "Dispatch, car 4067 is bringing in a prisoner. Bay one."

The swearing got louder as they approached the station. O'Brian threw himself back and forth in the seat. "That bitch, I'm gonna kill her, you just watch."

Hassim pulled into the bay and the door closed behind them. O'Brian jumped forward, but Hassim and Ferguson got out of the car. Ferguson videoed O'Brian as he kicked and screamed like a two year old throwing a tantrum.

"We're going to have to get the car detailed again." Hassim leaned against the wall and watched until O'Brian wound down. The door to processing opened.

"You've got a live one there." Constable Fianl shook her head. "I've called for backup in processing. Don't want it messed up now that I've got it the way I want."

Two more constables came through the door.

"Come with us, sir. We don't want you getting hurt." One of them opened the door and stepped back. "If you will get out of the car, we'll get you changed and cleaned up." O'Brian slid out of the car and hung his head. The constables led him into processing.

"I haven't charged him yet, so you can charge him with destruction of police property and give him his rights." Ferguson sighed and rolled his eyes. "I'm going to go see if there are any cars available."

"I'll get maintenance to pick up this one for cleaning." Hassim followed Ferguson through the door, into processing where Constable Fianl was taking mug shots. Ferguson buzzed through the door into the rest of the station.

"I'm arresting you. David O'Brian, you are charged with uttering threats and destruction of police property. You have the right to stay silent." Hassim went through the rights, but guessed he had heard them before. She headed to her desk to fill out the paperwork and call maintenance. She'd just finished up with maintenance when Ferguson came over.

He dangled a set of keys. "We'll have to drive a cruiser until our car is ready again."

"Oh joy." Hassim said. "It will be at least 24 hours, maybe more if he broke something. I'm going to get caught up with the paperwork." She turned to her desk and booted her computer.

***

Molly packed up the files and put them in a drawer of her desk in the bedroom. Her mind was half congealed glue.

Her phone rang and she picked up. "Hello."

"You sound like you've been up all night." Ciara sounded worried. "What's going on?"

"I just got up early and worked all morning on something."

"What? It must be important if you spent half your Sunday on it."

"I'm not allowed to talk about it." Molly said and waited for the reaction.

"It's about that phone call, isn't it?" Ciara's worry deepened. "You're all right?"

"I'm fine, it's just that I picked up some extra work and wanted to get a good start on it."

"That wasn't your work that called."

"No, it wasn't." Molly flopped on her bed. "I'm doing some analysis for the RCMP."

"What!" Ciara squeaked. "You're working with the cops?"

"Yes, but I can't say any more than that."

"It's not dangerous, is it?" Ciara whispered.

"I promise, it isn't dangerous." Molly yawned.

"I won't tell anyone." Ciara said. "You get some rest and call me when you get up."

"Okay." Molly disconnected the call and closed her eyes. Maybe just a short nap.

***

Ferguson sighed and pushed back from the table. "Do you have a lawyer you wish to call, or should I get the duty council?"

"I have a lawyer." O'Brian said with a shadow of his earlier bravado.

Ferguson led O'Brian to the secure line they had for prisoners to call out. "Call your lawyer and get them over here. We have some questions for you, and they can't wait."

"And if I don't want to answer them?" O'Brian's chin shoved forward.

"I believe your court date for threatening Ms. Callister is in a month." Ferguson opened the door. "I can make a good case to have the crown call you a flight risk. You have no home and no reason to stay in the community."

"That bitch can't do this me."

"That is a civil matter. Your lawyer will be able to explain." Ferguson frowned. "You have twenty minutes on the phone. If you need more, you will need to let the duty officer know."

When he was called back to the interview room, he found O'Brian with a middle-aged woman in a suit.

"My client wishes to cooperate with the police, but he won't answer any questions that might incriminate him."

"Fine with me." Ferguson turned on the video. "November 28th. Sergeant Ferguson interviewing David O'Brian with counsel present."

"Sergeant Hassim."

Ferguson nodded at the lawyer to introduce herself.

"Betty Poulson, representing David O'Brian."

Ferguson took out his notebook. "Mr. O'Brian, I have some questions for you about Friday night of November 26th." O'Brian's jaw hung open. "What?"

Ms. Poulson put a hand on his arm.

"This is not the direction my client expected the interview to take. I will have to confer with him."

"Knock on the door when you're done." Ferguson left the room and fetched a coffee. The knock came quicker than he expected. When he entered O'Brian looked deflated.

"My client is prepared to be completely forthcoming, in exchange for a more lenient sentence."

"That isn't up to the police, but if he cooperates, we will be sure to make that known to the Crown."

She looked O'Brian and he shrugged.

"Very well then ask your questions."

"You were in Riverside Park on Friday the 26th of November."

O'Brian nodded.

"Please answer out loud for the video record."

"Yes. My buddies and I were there."

"What was your purpose?" Ferguson leaned forward.

O'Brian hung his head.

"What was your purpose in going to the park that night?" Ferguson repeated evenly.

"We were going to find a homeless person and teach them a lesson." O'Brian mumbled.

"Please answer loud enough for the video to record."

"We was going to find someone and beat the shit out of them." O'Brian shouted.

"Did you see anyone else at the park that evening?"

"What?" O'Brian looked at him slack-jawed.

"Did you see anyone else at the park that evening?"

"No, but Tom had the creeps like someone was watching."

"What is Tom's last name?" Ferguson poised his pen over the booklet.

O'Brian looked at Ms. Poulson and she nodded.

"Henley, Thomas Henley."

"Thank you." Ferguson met O'Brian's eyes. "Anyone else there?" He let the silence stretch as O'Brian squirmed in his seat.

"Do I have to say? He'll be so mad at me."

Ferguson waited. The quiet in the room became like a living creature, stalking around the table.

"Bob Rook." O'Brian said and dropped his head on his hands.

"Were those the two who were with you when you threatened Ms. Callister on the street?"

"Yes." O'Brian lifted his head to speak then dropped it again. "I'm so dead."

"Did you know it was going to snow that night?"

"Bob knew; he was the planner. I'm not good at that stuff."

"Even if she hadn't been struck by an unknown assailant," Ferguson hardened his voice. "The coroner said she probably would have died before morning. How does it feel to be in debt to a killer?"

"It was supposed to be just pushing around and scaring her, but it got out of control."

"Who struck the first blow?"

"I did. It was my fault; I can never hold my temper when I've been drinking."

"Were Henley and Rook drinking too?"

"Damn right they were. They just laughed after I smacked her and jumped in."

Hassim left as Ferguson went over his questions a few more times, but O'Brian kept his answers consistent.

"I will get your statement typed up and a constable will bring it in for you to sign. I expect your counsel will want to read it before you sign." He stood and left the room. Hassim sat at the computer in the neighbouring room typing quickly.

"Just finishing up." She printed the page and passed it to Ferguson.

He checked it over and nodded. She always did good work. He stepped out and passed the page to a constable. "Take this into the prisoner in Interview 2. Once he's signed it, take him back to holding. Tell them to keep a close eye on him."

The constable nodded and knocked on the door of the interview room.

Ferguson followed Hassim to her desk. "What do you think?"

"He's as pathetic an excuse for a human being as I've ever seen." Hassim dropped into her chair and breathed slowly. After a dozen breaths she looked up at Ferguson. "I think he is telling the truth. He didn't try to fob responsibility off on his friends. I doubt either of his friends saw anyone. They sound like the group to run down a potential witness and threaten to silence."

"Agreed." Ferguson's stomach growled. "We'll take my car. We don't want to start any rumours." He let dispatch know they were going to eat.

"They know at Kamloops Correctional to pick him up?"

"I called earlier. They said later this evening."

"Great, let's get out of here." Hassim strode to the doors. "I need nourishment."

***

He climbed into his car, eager for the hunt. Tonight, he couldn't pretend to neutrality. He drove like everyone else on the road, just cautious enough to not crash, but not to pull attention to himself. North on Hwy 5 to Halston, then to Schubert. He parked well away from access to the beach. Walking with the bar held against his leg no longer felt awkward. It was a quick walk to the slope down to the beach. He'd been here years ago, but his memory was good. The dark trees on his left were dark, but the expanse of white on his right made just enough light for him to see.

The person bumped into him and shoved him aside. Adrenaline rushed like fire through his veins as he pivoted and brought the bar down on the shadow's head. The person grunted and fell on their face.

"Hey, what's going on?" A voice shouted at him. A woman, short but blocky was obscured behind a blinding light.

He ran into the trees and found a path. Running away would be the smartest thing to do, but she'd shone that damned light on him. She knew what he looked like. That couldn't be allowed. As the light made it progress toward him swung wildly. He ducked low and run in the direction she'd come from. If he could get behind her, it would be simple to strike her down.

She shouted something, must have found the person. He expected she'd climb the bank and go to a house to ask for help. Instead, she bolted back in the direction she'd come. The light became a diffuse glow. She'd crawled into a tent making it glow.

"I'm going to hunt you down, you bastard." From the rustling in the tent, she was looking for something. He had a feeling if she found it, he'd be in trouble. He ran to the small camp intending to attack her before she climbed out of the tent.

He knocked over a can of naphtha fuel and without thinking about it snatched it up and sloshed fuel over the tent. Matches lay on the ground beside an old camp stove. He struck a match and tossed it onto the tent. It lit up with a whoosh. He stuffed the matches in his pocket.

The screams he expected never came. She roared like a bear and burst up out of the tent waving a machete. He threw the can at her, but she beat it aside with her blade and rushed him. He didn't have time to pick up his bar, so he yanked the tank from the stove and pointed it at her. It hissed and gas hit her face, so she missed her slash and sliced open his coat instead of his gut. He ducked to the side and grabbed his bar almost dropping it again in his panic.

She wiped her face and glared at him. "I'm going to fucking kill you, then let you burn in that fire. You hurt Jack." Her lunge almost got him, but he instinctively beat the machete aside. She attacked again raging at him. It wouldn't be long before someone heard the racket and called the police. He had no time.

The matches. He let go of the bar with one hand and pulled them out he lit one and stood ready to throw it at her.

"That won't stop me from killing you." She bared her teeth and raised her huge knife and crouched ready to charge again. The match was almost burning his fingers. He lit the rest of the matchbook as she ran toward him. His throw fell well short, and he retreated, holding the bar like a sword in front of him. Her foot splashed in the puddle of gas on the ground. The splash made it back to the matches. The naphtha flamed up her clothes. She tried to wipe the flames away from her face, letting go of the machete.

He rushed in to attack but she pushed the bar aside with her left arm and punched him in the face. Pain exploded and he stumbled back. She kept swinging, batting the weak swings of the bar to the side. He tightened his grip. This time he aimed at the arm she used to push the bar away.

The crunch of bones made him sick, but he couldn't stop. He had no time for weakness. The woman bent forward. He jumped forward and brought the bar down on her head like an ax. She dropped to the ground, her clothes still with small flames flickering on her arms and legs. He picked up the can and dropped it on her. The gas blazed up as he fled the light.

By the time he'd reached the slope past his car and limped back to it, the pain in his face and arms was making him whimper. The coat and the bar he tossed in the trunk, then falling into the car, pushed the start button. It silently moved out onto the street, he took the first turn toward Fortune, then drove to Halston and took the highway the long way around to return to his house. As the automatic garage door closed behind him, he cried against the steering wheel.

It might have been minutes or hours later when he climbed out of the car and dragged himself inside. He stood in the shower until the hot water ran out, then inspected his face in the mirror.

He glared at his reflection. "I'm done."  But it didn't answer.

# CHAPTER 15
## Monday November 29

Ferguson hated early morning calls, he had to struggle to orient himself to what day it was. The fire department had their equipment out making sure the fire really had burned itself out. The fire captain came over to Ferguson.

"This is a mess."

"No kidding." Ferguson forced his tone to be light. It wasn't Frank's fault they had to follow protocol, that meant sacrificing the crime scene for public safety.

"We have someone alive." A shout came from the bottom of the bank.

Ferguson and the fire captain stiffened and looked at each other. Rescue dragged a stretcher cage down the slope. The firefighters moved out of the way. Twenty minutes later they carried the stretcher up the slope. Working as if they were on a mountain, not a fifteen foot bank. No short cuts, everything by the numbers.

Ferguson walked over to the ambulance as they secured him for the ride. He was a young man, thin and worn by the street, but Ferguson didn't see any signs of drug use. The young man's clothes were drenched in blood, his head bandaged, and blood had already seeped through the layers of gauze, but his chest moved up and down as he breathed.

"What do you think about his chances?" Ferguson asked one of the rescue team.

"Can't say." The woman looked over at the Ambulance as it headed on its run to the Royal Inland Hospital. "He's a tough one."

"The scene is yours." The fire captain called to Ferguson.

He clambered down to where the remains of a person lay sprawled on their back. Their torso was burnt black, the hands lay unburned in the snow. Even with the face charred, he could see the skull was crushed in. Ferguson crouched to get a closer look. The left arm had a bend where it shouldn't have. The victim tried to defend themselves. A machete lay in the snow not far from the body. The thing that twisted his gut was the square can lying on the body. The label was unreadable, but a red naphtha tank and a stove told him what it was. The killer had poured gas on the body, then placed the can and lit it.

Maybe it was a reaction to her fighting back? The scene of crime people would be all over the place in minute. He was breaking protocol by looking first and adding more contamination. The firefighter's boots had flattened the area around the body and a burnt tent. A trail led into the darkness where they'd found the young man. He followed it until he came on the depression where the victim had fallen. Ferguson shone his flashlight around the area and saw black specks on the snow.

He walked back to the scene stepping carefully around the photographers to the woman coordinating the team.

"They found a second victim on the beach." Ferguson pointed into the darkness. "I think there may be blood trail. I'd like to know where it goes."

"I'll put someone on it." She made notes on her clipboard. "You think the kid will make it?"

"Don't know." Ferguson shrugged. "Not my job."

"That's a bit cold." The woman said.

"I want him to live as much as anyone. But keeping him alive isn't my work. I'm here to catch the killer and make sure that young man is remembered as himself, not victim number six."

"I'll get to work." She turned to talk to a member of her team.

Ferguson clambered up the ladder that made improvised steps up to Schubert St. He called Hassim and left a voice message. He hadn't known it was one of his cases until he saw the crushed skull.

"We have another one, but this time there might be a witness. I'm going up to the hospital to keep track of how the survivor is doing." He climbed into his cruiser and let dispatch know where he was headed.

At the RIH he parked and walked into Emergency, putting a mask on, and sanitized his hands.

"The young man who came in by ambulance from Schubert St. Who is someone I can talk to about his condition?" Ferguson held out his badge. The man scrutinized the ID, then handed it back.

"He'll be in surgery. There will be someone there to give you what information we can."

"Thanks." Unfortunately, Ferguson didn't need any guide to the surgery waiting room. He was the only one there. The dim light made all the colours look grey.

"Hello Sergeant Ferguson." A nurse in green scrubs came over to him. "All we have right now is he's stable. No idea what issues may arise once he wakes up."

"Thanks. I'll wait for an update."

The nurse looked around the depressing room.

"He should have someone waiting for him." Ferguson sat down and took out his phone. "I can do some work from here."

Four twenty-seven in the morning the nurse came out to Ferguson.

"He's awake."

"Great, let me know when he will be able to talk to me."

"He wants to see you now. First thing he said when he opened his eyes."

Ferguson put away his phone and stood up. "Let's not keep him waiting."

As they walked to the recovery room the surgeon met them.

"He's asking for you, Sergeant, but keep in mind he'll be confused. He sustained a moderately severe head injury. He's lucky he took a glancing blow." She met his gaze without looking away.

"I won't keep him long." Ferguson said. "I will come back tomorrow when he is more conscious and alert. This is as much for him as me."

"Very well." The surgeon left and the nurse showed Ferguson into the room.

"Hello, I'm Sergeant Ferguson, you wanted to speak to me?"

"I need to talk to a cop." The young man slurred his speak.

"I'm a cop." Ferguson showed the kid his badge. "What's your name?"

"He killed Queenie. The devil did. He tried to strike me down, but God saved me. I don't know why. I'm Jack."

"You will find out in time." Ferguson said. "Can you tell me what the devil looked like?"

"He was tall, taller than Queenie, he had a sword he used to beat her down." Jack's lip curled up microscopely. "But Queenie gave him a fight. She was about to win when he lit her on fire, then cut her head off with his sword."

Ferguson noted everything down word for word. He could winnow it later to find a clue.

Tears ran down Jack's cheeks. "Queenie was a hard ass, but she took care of me. I should have died with her."

"You're alive, so you'll need to find a way to live for her." Ferguson put his notebook away. "I will come back later today or tomorrow when you're more awake and able to talk."

Jack closed his eyes, and the nurse showed him out of the room.

"I wish he could have been more useful."

"He saw something and interpreted so he could understand it. His information is invaluable."

"I'll let him know later." The nurse walked Ferguson out to the waiting room. "I'll keep you posted about how he's doing."

"Thanks." Ferguson decided to go home and try to get a few hours sleep before starting tomorrow. He shook head. Today.

***

Molly dragged herself out of bed. She'd slept most of Sunday, then through the night. Caffeine would wake her up. Her phone blinked at her. Someone sent left her a voice message. Most people sent texts. She picked up the phone and listened to the message as she lurched toward the bathroom.

"Ferguson here. There was another one early this morning. Anything you can tell be about Jack and Queenie would be very helpful."

His words hit her like a bucket of cold water. Molly wanted to curl up and hide, she wanted to scream. Instead, she took a shower and dressed, then went and put the coffee maker on. Blue had already left for work. Damn she needed a hug. That reminded her she hadn't talked to Tad yet. She sent him a quick message to call her in the evening to talk about the movie. Breakfast first, then she'd call Ferguson with what she knew so far.

"Ferguson."

"It's Molly, I got your message."

"You have something already?" She could almost hear the lift in his eyebrows.

"Just what I know from working with them. I will have to get permission to share information from their files."

"Call me if you run into trouble. Now what do you have for me?"

"Jack aged out of foster care a few years ago and ended up on the street. He got lucky and was picked up by Queenie. She's no angel. Most people avoid her, but Jack did everything she told him to. He's never said, but reading between the lines that included sex. The harder she was on him the more he worshipped her."

"Any background on Queenie?"

"Not a lot, she doesn't like talking to people like me. I'll see what's in her file. I know she showed up about five years back, but I couldn't tell you from where."

"That's helpful. At least we have a firm ID on her."

"I wish I could figure out who that man and woman were."

"If you know, that's helpful, but it isn't part of your job."

"Thanks." Molly poured herself a coffee. "I'll talk to you as soon as I've spoken to my supervisor."

After eating her breakfast, she booted up her computer and checked the news. Nothing in it about the incident this morning.

She found an article by Cheryl.

I spent some time with Molly Callister, a street social-worker and got a crash course on homelessness. To be honest I was prepared to hear awful stories and to be told how hard it is to survive on the street. I wasn't prepared for the lessons I learned from Molly.

Walking down the street Molly was almost immediately stopped by a woman. The woman wanted help right away, and I expected to see some social work in action. But Molly could only try to connect her to resources. The woman wanted furniture for a place she was moving into. Even having an apartment doesn't make a home if there is no furniture to make it a home. What is the incentive to work on your life only to spend it in a bare room?

There are so many people who need help that it takes a team effort to work with them. Molly passed the woman's name and need to a worker at The Loop. We sat and had coffee and a tiny bit of breakfast. We sat with, I'll call him Eeyore, and Molly talked about why The Loop calls people who come through their door guests. They aren't problems to be fixed. The woman we met in different circumstances could be a customer wanting to speak the manager, not happy with the service she's getting.

Eeyore announced three people who had died in the past three days. He said it would be a hard winter. Molly asked if he had a safe place to sleep. He said there was no safe place.
Through the day I watched Molly talk with people compassionately, but recognizing each person's need to do what they can. I was shocked at first, but the more we went through the day, the more I realized that

given a choice, I would like Molly to be the one working with me.

Her mantra was 'There is no 'us' and 'them'.' Every time I would talk about the homeless as a group, she challenged me to see individual people with unique stories and needs. It was a hard lesson, but one I've decided I'm glad to have learned.

That woman who wanted furniture? I arranged through The Loop to give her some of the stuff gathering dust in my storage locker. Not because I was sorry for the woman, but because that's the kind of person I like to think I am.

Cheryl went on to list the agencies offering services and how one could make a donation or get involved. She talked about how the winter was especially difficult for people living without a home.

Molly couldn't decide if she was pleased or horrified with the article. Don would have something to say about it. She'd wait until then to decide.

She went straight to his office and knocked on the door.

"Molly, I was expecting to see you this morning. Have a seat."

Molly perched on the chair waiting for the tirade to begin.

"Over all I liked Cheryl's article. You didn't give her the experience I expected, but from what she wrote it was what she needed. I think will be helpful. I like the emphasis on working with the individual not a member of a group."

Molly sighed and relaxed in her chair.

"If that is everything?" Don looked at her obviously expecting her to leave and get ready for the briefing.

"I have taken on a temporary position with the RCMP as a consultant in regards to the homeless. Sergeant Ferguson said you could call him to get more information."

Don made a note. "Don't get in over your head."

"I am working hard on sticking to what they've asked me to do, which brings up a request. I'd like to access the files to help in identifying and getting background on certain individuals."

"This is about the killings the last few days?"

"I can't answer that." Molly looked at her feet.

"I see." Don steepled his fingers and peered at her. "I will call the executive director and see what she says about the files. If you need to talk, I'm here."

Molly opened her mouth to explain again about the not being able to talk, but Don raised his hand.

"I know you said you can't talk about your work, but you are able to talk about what that work is doing to you."

"Thank you." Molly stood up. "It's hard, but I'm holding it together. I will keep in mind that your door is always open."

Don nodded and she walked from the office not sure how she felt. He didn't mind the article, and he could be an ear to listen when she needed it.

She didn't know whether to be relieved or disappointed that she wasn't assigned to Schubert St. It was probably just as well.

Through the day she found both Zeke and Edwin. She learned from Zeke the woman was named Olivia and she had husband and children before alcohol destroyed her life. Edwin warned her the streets would get more dangerous before they got better.

"It may be time for me to move on. With this much attention the risk of them finding me is too great."

"Okay." Molly nodded. "Call me if you need help."

She spent the day meandering along Victoria West to the Café. A tall man, she thought his name was Dave, came over and sat at her table.

"You okay?" He stared at her. "That guy you met at Tim's looked pretty sketchy."

"I'm fine, he was just mentioning a job offer that might interest me." She sighed at Dave's doubtful gaze. "Really, it's a social work job. A little extra money to add to the part-time work I do now."

"Bad stuff happens around him." Dave frowned. "You be extra careful around him."

"I will." Molly stood. "I need to get back to the office. Thanks for the warning."

***

Don gave her limited access to the files.

"You check with me about each file you use and what information you need from it. Let me know what files you want."

"Actually, I have a name now." Molly held her breath. "Olivia."

"Let's take a look." Don stood up and led the way to the file room. Each file had a number, and the first thing she had to do was find the files for Olivia. Olivia was easy, there was only one of her. She looked through people on the North Shore. There were a few possibilities for the man in the sleeping bag. She carried the files to the office.

Molly read through them making notes as she went. One of the men's files was a man name Pat. His file was slim. He kept to himself, but visited The Loop on occasion. One of the workers had recently found him a new pair of boots. They'd been donated by a big box store. The record even named the brand of boot. The others she found were also loners with thin files.

Olivia's file was thicker and sadder. She'd been in and out of rehab many times. Each time she'd determine to stay sober, but without a change in her environment it was hard for her to avoid the alcohol. She'd tattooed the names of her children on her arm to make sure she never forgot them.

When she'd phoned Ferguson she got his voice mail, so she told him she had information for him. Then headed home.

A car pulled up beside her on Vernon and Molly's heart thumped, then Tad jumped out.

"I figured you'd be walking along here." He leaned against the car.

"I asked you to call this evening."

"I couldn't wait." He smiled crookedly.

"What happened to you?" Molly stared at the bruises on his face.

Tad winced and looked sheepish. "Was at the bar the other night and got into a fight."

"Really." Molly stepped back. "You always told me you didn't like violence."

"Yeah, now I remember why."

"Well since you're here. Come by the usual time for the movie."

"I'd like to take you out for dinner." Tad looked down. "It's the least I can do after how I treated you."

"Okay then six o'clock will give me a chance to have a shower and change." Molly nodded and continued walking. It wasn't good weather for standing outside and chatting. At least that what she told herself. Tad's eyes made her back itch. She'd see him tomorrow, but she had to take time to get her head in the right space. Now that she'd decided to give him a chance, she needed to make it a proper chance.

Ferguson phoned just as she was walking into the apartment. She put down her messenger bag and hung the coat in the closet while balancing the phone on her shoulder.

"Give me a second to get settled." Molly carried the bag over to the table and pulled out the file she'd put together. "The male may be Patrick Chance. He kept to himself mostly, but got some cold weather gear at The Loop. They are a size 9 Sorel. Almost new. I don't have anything on the coat other than it might have been blue. The woman may be Olivia Standish. She had the names of her children tattooed on her arm. Paul, Thomas, and Gracie are the names. I can give you the emergency contact information for Olivia if you need it. I have nothing on Pat's family."

"That's great." Ferguson said. "Two people last night, the killer may be escalating. Jack is alive but is the hospital under care. He said Queenie laid a beating on the killer, then they shot fire at them and beheaded her."

"That's horrible." Molly's stomach cringed.

"She wasn't beheaded, but from where he was and with his injuries it might have looked like it. There was fire involved. The torso and face of the body were charred, and the tent had burned. I'm thinking the killer used the tank from a naphtha stove as a mini flamethrower."

"That's not much better." Molly sat down and started making notes.

"Oh, he said it was the devil who killed her, all dressed in black."

"If they wore a balaclava it would look that way." Something creaked on Ferguson's end of the line. "I have a bit more news for you. You were right about the car. Scene of Crime followed a blood trail to where Jack was struck by the killer. The killer's footprints led to a parking spot on Schubert near the south end of the beach."

"That's something." Molly put her pen down.

"Oh, one more thing, that map you found us led us to arrest two of the three people who assaulted the woman in the park. The third one, Bob Rook, is a ghost. However long he's known these two, he's been using an alias. Both men in custody said Rook was the organizer and planner. This wasn't a once off attack."

"I think I've heard the name from work but can't connect who would have used it." Molly wrote the name on her pad.

"Let me know if you think of something."

"I will." Molly hung up and realized Blue wasn't in the apartment. She checked her phone, but there wasn't a message from him. Odd.

Molly put supper in the oven and set the table and Blue still hadn't shown up. Maybe he missed the bus or something. She sent him a text. 'Supper's on.'

Her phone rang a few minutes later and she answered hoping it was Blue.

"Hi Molly, I wanted to make sure you got home okay." Tad said. "You left pretty abruptly; you still mad at me?"

"Yes and no." Molly sat on the couch and wrapped the blanket around her. "I have decided to go out with you to the movies again, we'll see what happens from that. I need to get my head straight so I can be fair to you."

"Okay, what do you want to eat?"

"Haven't had Italian in a while." Molly switched the phone to the other ear. "I'll trust you to choose a place."

Here phone beeped showing an incoming call from Blue.

"I have to go, Blue's calling. Good night." She switched the call over to Blue. "Hey, I was beginning to worry about you."

"Someone jumped me in the alley. I was putting the garbage out." He groaned. "I'll live but will be sore for a good while."

"You still in the alley?" Molly jumped to her feet.

"By the bin." Blue groaned. "Someone's here with me. If they hadn't interrupted, it would have been a lot worse."

"I'll call Tad and come and get you, unless you want me to call 911?" Her chest was tight.

"I'll see you in a few minutes." Molly dialed Tad and prayed for him to pick up.

"Hello Molly, what's up?" Tad might have been puzzled or annoyed. Molly couldn't tell and she didn't care"

"Blue's hurt, behind the Café, someone's with him, but I need to get there as soon as I can."

"I can come, but I'm up in Aberdeen, it will take a while to get there."

"Crap." Molly stopped herself from throwing the phone against the wall.

"Look, I sent a taxi over to your place, should be there in a few minutes. I'll meet you in the alley."

"Thanks." Molly hung up and threw her coat and boots on. Grabbed her hat and gloves as an afterthought and ran down to the front of the building.

A taxi waited for her. *Already?* She dashed out to the car.

"You Molly Callister?" The driver asked when she nodded, he unlocked the doors, and she jumped in. The cab driver didn't waste any time getting on the road. He drove quickly but carefully through the sparse evening traffic. They arrived at the Café.

"Around back." Molly pointed. "There's an alley."

The driver took her around to the alley and Molly hardly waited for the car to stop before jumping out and running to where Blue sat against the wall. Edwin crouched beside him.

"Blue!" Molly wanted to hug him tightly, but it wasn't a good time. She didn't know what his injuries were. She settled for taking his hand and stroking it.

"Broke my own rules and this is what I get for it." Blue winced. "Supposed to have two people doing garbage after dark."

"What happened?" Molly asked.

"I was putting the garbage in the bin when someone jumped me, punched me in the lower back then smacked my head against the bin. I fell down and curled up tight. He was kicking me when Edwin shouted, and the guy ran off. He took my wallet and my phone, but swore at the phone and dropped it. There is something to be said for not having the latest tech."

"I couldn't see much. The guy was over six feet, maybe two hundred and fifty pounds. Wore black, made him hard to see." Edwin said.

"Thanks, I'm glad you were here." She heard a footstep behind her and whirled around ready to defend Blue, but the taxi driver stood hands up.

"Sorry didn't mean to startle you." The man said. "Mr. Willis said I was to check if you were okay before I left."

"Oh no." Molly smacked her forehead. "I didn't bring my purse with me. How much is it, and I'll send it to your company.

"No need. Mr. Willis put it on his account."

"Thank you." Molly stiffened her legs as they wanted to wobble. "You've been a lifesaver."

"Glad to help." The driver got into the taxi and drove off.

"Maybe we should get Blue inside," Edwin said. "It is cold out here and Blue doesn't have a coat on."

Between Molly and Edwin, they got Blue to his feet and made the short walk to the back door of the Café. After installing Blue in a chair. Edwin looked at Molly.

"If you are okay from here, I will get on my way." He sighed. "It has been a pleasure knowing you, but for your own safety, you won't see me again."

"I will miss our chats." Molly hugged him and he went still for a second.

"As will I." Edwin stepped back with his hands on Molly's shoulders. "Be safe, there are many dangerous people about. The worst of them don't look dangerous." He turned to walk out the back.

"Be careful, he may not have gone far." Molly said.

"No one will bother me." Edwin's smile looked sad.

Tad arrived minutes after Edwin left.

"Blue how are you? Should I drive you to the hospital or call an ambulance?" Tad crouched and looked at Blue's eyes. "Pupils are the same size, that's good, but you should have a doctor check you out."

"If you insist." Blue stood and Tad steadied him. They got him out to the car and Tad took them up to the hospital.

"We're going to be waiting a while," Molly said to Tad. "There's no need for you to hang around for hours. I will see you tomorrow." She gave him a hug and let him hold her for a while.

"I don't mind waiting with you." Tad sat beside her. "Waiting by yourself is awful."

Molly ended up leaning against Tad and sleeping before Blue was given the all clear.

"C'mon sleepy head." Tad shook her gently. "Time to get you and Blue home." He took her hand and led her and Blue to his car. Tad helped Molly into the front seat and Blue into the back before taking the driver's seat. He drove them to the apartment building and insisted on helping Blue up the stairs to their door.

"Thanks again." Molly suddenly felt awkward. Would he want another hug, a kiss? But Tad only smiled and left.

After seeing Blue settled in his room, Molly lay down in her bed and tried to sleep. As exhausted as she was, her eyes wouldn't stay closed.

# CHAPTER 16
**Tuesday November 30**

Molly didn't recall falling asleep, but the nightmare woke her up gasping with fear. The only image that stayed with her was Blue lying on the street with blood pouring from a crushed skull.

Molly got up and made some tea and toast, hoping the image would fade. When she'd finished her tea, she checked on Blue, then went back to bed. Before she tried to sleep, she phoned her work and told Don she wouldn't be in that day.

Noises from the kitchen woke her and she put on her robe and went to talk to Blue.

"How are you feeling?" He handed her a cup of coffee.

"Isn't that my line?" Molly sipped at the cup and sighed. "You had me terrified last night."

"Sorry." Blue poured himself a cup and sat at the table with a groan. "Lots of bruises but nothing that should slow me down, much."

"Do you think it's connected to the case?"

"Highly improbable." Blue rubbed his shoulder. "Your killer is after the homeless and uses a bar of some kind to crush their skulls. My skull is still complete, so it isn't them. More likely someone taking advantage of the push back against the homeless to try to make a statement. Even more likely it was a mugging and all they wanted was my wallet. That's slim pickings at the best of times."

"You should report it to the police anyway." Molly sat across from him.

"I did when I woke up. They'll send an officer around when one is available. I'm alive and relatively unhurt, so a low priority."

"I guess." Molly stared into her mug. Her phone rang. "Molly here."

"No murder last night." Ferguson said. "You were going to look up Queenie and Jack for me."

"I'm sorry." Molly blinked a few times. "Blue was mugged last night. I was up all night with worry."

"He okay?" Ferguson's voice softened.

"Just a few bruises, fortunately." Molly moved her mug. "He phoned the police, but they'll come by to take his statement when someone has time."

"Be happy," Ferguson said. "If you are a priority for the police, it means you or someone close to you is seriously messed up."

"Blue said the same thing."

"I'll come around with Hassim and take his statement. At the same time, we can bring you up to date with the case."

"I'll be here." Molly hung up and sighed. "My head feels like a cotton ball. I'm going to have a quick shower."

By the time she got out of the shower and dressed, Ferguson and Hassim were talking with Blue. They didn't have their notebooks out, so he must have finished with the statement.

"Sorry to keep you waiting." Molly sat on the couch.

"Only a few minutes." Hassim waved a mug of coffee. "No problem."

"Here's what we've learned since last time we talked. Your IDs were correct. We have contacted Olivia's family. Her husband said he'd expected the call since the last time she fell off the wagon." Ferguson leaned back. "I hate those calls, but you never know what you will learn from them."

"The tracks leading back to Schubert are the same boot pattern as we've found before. They aren't an unusual brand style, so even if we find someone with the same boots it isn't much in the way of evidence." Hassim frowned. "Jack is still alive and insisting the devil murdered Queenie. We are fortunate to have that much. A centimeter the wrong way and he'd be dead."

"I don't expect he feels lucky just yet." Molly said. "He has no one to run to, and he lost his protector."

"That's hard, but he's made it this far." Ferguson looked at her. "Maybe the people at your work can help him."

"If he's willing to be helped, we'll certainly do what we can."

"Speaking of Jack, he's right. Queenie landed more than a few punches. Her knuckles were split and bloody. Given the timing it has to be a fight with the killer."

"So the killer must be in bad shape." Molly leaned her head back. "Bruised face maybe some other damage."

"I don't know how many people are walking around with bruised faces." Hassim shook her head. "It isn't so useful unless we have a specific suspect. They were probably feeling bad and took a night off. Or maybe they were busy with other things and didn't have time."

"Right. So what next?" Molly rolled her shoulders and looked at Ferguson.

"I see two possibilities." Ferguson held up a finger. "First is they decide they've had enough and stop and get rid of any evidence of their actions. We'll never find them if they do that." He held up the second. "The other is that they return to killing, but escalate it to multiple victims in a night or takes some action that would cause a lot of deaths. We won't know for sure until they kill again."

"That's terrible." Molly sipped from her mug and cupped her hands around it for warmth.

"Most murders are by people the victim knows. Tracking them down is often a matter of examining the people in that person's life. But random killings like this are hard to solve unless the killer makes a serious mistake." Ferguson frowned. "I don't like hoping for another death, but that is realistically the only way we'll catch this person."

"I can understand why police officers stick with a case for years." Molly glanced over at Blue, but he looked fine. "I would hate not ever getting answers."

"It happens." Ferguson shook his head. "You can't let it eat you up. Move on to the next case and deal with that one." He stood. "I've taken enough of your time."

Molly took the cups from Ferguson and Hassim. "I'm going out for dinner and a movie tonight, so please don't call unless it is urgent."

"We'll have no need to call unless there is another victim." Ferguson smiled at her. "Enjoy your night out."

***

Peter looked at his feet. The dealership was in trouble. With his father's shares and money tied up in probate his cash flow would be tight. His mom would help as much as she could. In the movies it didn't take a year or more to execute a will. Damn that man to hell. Why'd he have to kill father? Another year and Peter's investments would have been diversified enough to survive until the inheritance came. The timing couldn't have been worse.

The phone buzzed and Peter picked it up.

"Hi Peter, sorry about your father. He was a stand-up businessman. Unfortunately, you are an unknown. I am planning on consolidating my investments. I will need you to buy out my share of the dealership."

Peter's mouth hung open in shock. The timing couldn't be worse.

"Give me some time, and I will put together the money."

"Don't take too long." The caller hung up and Peter threw the phone against the wall. He was deliberately trying to drive Peter into the red. The dealership was on the line and all his father's assets were tied up in probate. He walked over to the phone and ground it under his foot. The cleaning service were coming today, they'd clean it up.

His hands shook as if looking for someone to throttle. A few of his friends knew people on the grey side of the business world. If he could borrow enough, he might be able to make it work.

Pearl and Vikrant were useless, neither of them cared about business, and his mother would council patience.

He couldn't be patient. Peter Bajwa would be known as man who made his own fortune, not inherited it from his father. Tearing out of the garage, Peter reached to switch off the radio, but he heard something that made him stop. For the first time that day, he smiled. A newscaster talked about the security company hired by the city, and the controversy over the violent reaction of one of the guards. The city was planning on expanding the use of security guards and some people worried about how they'd be held accountable.

Peter had sold a used truck to Sam Willis just before he'd been fired from the security company. Because of the name, the address on the form stuck in his mind. The man was exactly the kind of person who would know how to get his hands on a gun. He drove over to Sam's place. The truck was parked in the driveway. Peter parked behind the truck and went to knock on the door.

***

The only problem with taking a day off work was the boredom. Molly had gone over the files twice more but gleaned nothing from them. There was no connection between the victims aside from them being homeless and vulnerable.

Only four o'clock, still too early to start getting ready. Maybe Ciara would be home from school.

Ciara answered the phone.

"Tonight's the big night." Ciara teased her.

"Yeah." Molly said.

"You don't sound happy about it."

Molly flopped on the couch. "Maybe I shouldn't have taken the day off work."

"Why'd you do that?" Molly could hear the eyes rolling.

"Blue got mugged last night. I couldn't sleep. Then the police were here, and I didn't think I could handle it.

"What did Blue do?"

"He had meetings to attend."

Ciara laughed. "Have you decided what you're wearing?"

"Not yet, I was hoping you had some advice."

"What kind of look are you wanting?" Ciara switched to all business. "You want to look good, but not so good you make him look ridiculous if he doesn't dress up. From what you've said Tad is pretty casual."

"True, but I think he may dress up a bit tonight. We're going for supper and a movie."

"What are you eating?"

"Something Italian." Molly shook her head. "That could be anything from pizza to high cuisine."

"Maybe something red?"

"Right. I don't think so, but not white." Molly stood and walked to her room and opened the closet, switching the camera on the phone so it showed her clothes. She tried one outfit and another until she was exhausted. "Why can I never do this?" Molly fell onto her bed.

"Let's try another angle." Ciara said. "Do you want him to know what he almost lost, or that you want him back?"

"Where do you learn this stuff?" Molly rolled onto her stomach.

"Romance movies." Ciara snorted. "Though who really has that many clothes?"

"I know I don't." Molly sighed. "We've tried every combination already."

"But we were asking the wrong question. Stay with me." Ciara made her voice pleading and Molly laughed.

They went through the clothes again and finally settled on clothes Molly thought would work. She laid them on her bed. A green turtleneck, black dress pants. Even Ciara didn't think a skirt made sense in this weather. Molly found a gold chain with an opal pendant one of the Pointy Shoe Lades gave her. She'd wear her dressier boots, though they weren't as warm.

Molly had her shower and dried off before Blue came in. She dressed and went to meet him.

"You been talking to Ciara?" Blue lifted his eyebrows.

"Of course." Molly rolled her eyes. "I'm helpless with this stuff."

"You're learning." He hung up his coat and put his boots on the mat. "You aren't taking a purse?"

"I was going to carry my wallet and phone in my coat pocket." Molly tried to think if she even owned a purse other than her messenger bag.

"No problem." Blue winked. "I don't think Tad is going to notice."

Molly's phone buzzed. She checked the message.

"I'm here. I have the car, but I can leave it parked if you want to take the bus."

Molly thought about her not so warm boots.

"Let's take the car." Molly pushed away her misgivings and reached for her boots. "I'll be down in a few minutes."

As she left the building Molly saw Tad leaning against a car and waving.

"This is a different car." Molly looked it over. "It's blue and smaller."

Tad opened the door for her. "One of my father's companies leases a fleet of cars. I get to pick a different one every year. I just switched cars."

"A new car every year?" The idea boggled Molly's mind.

"Not quite." Tad closed his door and started the car. "This is two or three years old. It will get retired at the end of the fiscal year and I'll have to drive a different one."

"You sound disappointed."

"I like the car." Tad shrugged, "but it isn't up to me. He pushed a button to start the car, put it in gear and drove smoothly through the traffic.

"What's the difference between this car and the other ones? Why do you like this one?"

"It's hard to say." Tad drove down Fortune. "It makes me feel good when I drive it."

"And other cars don't?" Molly tried to understand how a car could make someone feel good and not another.

"Most of them are just cars. They get me from here to there. This one is like a favourite pair of shoes, it's more comfortable."

"I can understand the favourite shoes."

Tad navigated to Victoria St. and found a parking spot.

"I have a reservation at Peter's Pasta." Tad helped her out of the car. "Careful, the sidewalk is a bit slippery."

It was natural to hold onto Tad's arm as they walked to the restaurant. The hostess met them and took them to a table and left menus. Under his coat, Tad wore a dress shirt she thought had to be worth more than a week of her salary.

Molly looked through the menu and wondered how she was going to decide.

"Order whatever you want." Tad was looking through the menu. "I think I'm going to have the Sockeye Salmon."

"I don't know. There's too much choice." Molly sighed.

"Take your time. Pick something that sounds good. We can't eat through the whole menu in one visit."

Molly laughed and settled on the Lasagna Al Forno. They ordered their meals and Tad ordered Bruschetta to start.

"Tell me about the fight." Molly asked, then could have kicked herself.

Tad sighed and shook his head. "I was in a bad mood and went out to a bar with a few friends and drank too much. I learned that I'm not as tough as I like to think I am." He touched the bruises on his face. "I got off lightly, the other guy wasn't interested in destroying me. I paid for the damages and picked up the other guy's tab as an apology. My friends took me home and I put a bag of frozen peas on my face."

"Everyone makes stupid mistakes." Molly smiled at him. "It's what we learn from them that counts."

"Is that a way of asking if I've learned anything from you?" Tad took a long drink of water. "I liked the idea of being the big strong protector but that isn't what you need. You talked that guy in the coffee shop out of a fight, you didn't blink when you were faced with that neanderthal on the street. I would have made things worse."

"So, what are you going to be instead of the protector?" Molly tilted her head.

"Honestly, I don't know. I've spent the last week trying to figure out who I am under all the money and tough guy image."

The bruschetta arrived and Tad insisted Molly try it. The tomato and garlic worked well with the bread. The conversation turned to the food, and they chatted about it while they ate, trading bites of their dinners.

Tad paid the bill without blinking, though Molly tallied up how many hours of work she would need to pay for it.

They walked along Victoria to the theatre and arrived in time to pick up drinks and popcorn before they went in.

The movie was a romantic comedy about a rich man who meets a cashier from a grocery store. They had all the usual misunderstandings and problems with their families before they had a fight about the man's money. She went back to being a cashier but wasn't happy. It ended with the man getting a job at the store and living off what he made. They had their happy ever after as they moved into a nice apartment, and he kept his money as a safety net.

"I don't think the problem was his money." Molly said as they sat in the coffee shop. "He had no purpose beyond being rich. She was better off than him, because she knew who she wanted to be."

"She had her problems too." Tad added. "Once she knew he was rich, the money is all she worried about."

"You're right." Molly sipped her coffee. "Money is a hard thing to ignore. We're told that money can't buy happiness, but the lack of it brings on a boatload of misery."

"I'll have to trust your word, that's never been a problem for me. I don't talk at the Loop or Café much because I don't know what to talk about."

"You can't go wrong with listening to what people want to tell you." Molly made a face. "There's the social worker in me coming out."

"Is that a bad thing?" Tad stirred his cappuccino.

"If it is an easy out, it is." Molly frowned. "I like my job, but I think I've been trying to be more social worker than Molly. I don't have many friends outside of my work and my family. It was the same at school, the only person who might have been a friend..."

"That was hard, but it wasn't your fault." Tad leaned forward and took her hand. "Some people just don't want to be fixed."

"I don't think anyone wants to be fixed." Molly wiped her eyes with her other hand. "It is more about being prepared to do the hard things to grow than having people fix you. I'm not broken, well not completely, and every time I put myself together, I learn more about who I'm supposed to be."

"That doesn't sound like much fun." Tad squeezed her hand. "I think you are fine just as you are."

Molly blinked back tears. "You don't know me that well. Not your fault, I never really let you see me."

Tad tilted his head and stared at Molly until she started tearing up again. "I never got to tell you how beautiful you are."

Molly stared at him. "Ciara helped me choose the outfit."

"I'm not talking about your outfit. I'm talking about you." Tad handed her a napkin.

"I'm not beautiful." Molly shook in her chair. "You know what I was."

"I do." Tad said. "I'm not in love with your past, but you."

Molly's heart skipped a beat. "Love?"

Tad turned a deep red. "Sorry that just slipped out." He looked down. "But it's true."

She turned away and thought of the people she could say she loved. Blue, Ciara, Hanna. People who knew her scars and didn't care. No, not that they didn't care, but they looked past them to who she was.

"Who am I?" Molly whispered. "I thought I knew."

"Same here." Tad said. "Being with you changes who I thought I was."

"I think I need to go home before I fall apart." Molly stood and put her coat on. "Thank you for the meal and the movie."

Tad got up. "I'll drive you home."

"I can take the bus, please."

"It isn't safe." Tad took her hand, but she pulled away.

"Sorry." Molly ran out of the coffee shop barely able to see through the tears. *What am I doing?* She didn't have an answer. The street was deserted. *I should call Hanna.* It was late, she didn't want to bother her friend and what explanation could she give? Molly shook her head. She was being stupid, and Hanna would be furious with her.

Molly's feet carried her along 7th Ave toward Lansdowne. She wasn't far from the alley where that businessman had been murdered. Something moved in the dark alley. Molly stopped to look and heard a moan. She pulled out her phone and dialed 911 and asked for police.

"Someone's hurt in the alley between Victoria and Lansdowne."

"In what city?"

"Kamloops." Molly gasped for air. Was someone coming out of the alley?

"I'll put you through."

"Kamloops RCMP, where are you?"

Molly's words tumbled out and she had to repeat herself. Footsteps sounded, getting closer to her. A flashlight blinded her

"I know you." A voice spoke from the dark behind the light.

Her hands trembled so violently she couldn't hold onto the phone. It clattered on the sidewalk, and she scrambled for it. She had to get away, so she ran, slipped on the ice, and crashed to the ground. Sirens wailed as she tried to get up, but her bad ankle hurt too much. Molly pushed herself against the wall and looked around in panic. Her chest burned and her right arm twinged.

A figure came out of the alley, picked up her phone and disappeared again.

The police came a few minutes later and called an ambulance for her. Molly's teeth chattered made it hard to talk. Another car arrived and two officers walked down the alley with their flashlights on. Minutes later more cars arrived. Ferguson and Hassim climbed out and talked to the first cop to arrive. Hassim came over and crouched beside Molly.

"You'll be okay, it's shock."

"He,he t,took my ph, phone." Molly stuttered.

The ambulance arrived and Hassim let the paramedics do their work.

"We're going to take you up to the hospital and let them assess you. Shock is hitting you hard and it needs to be monitored." They loaded her on the gurney and put it in the ambulance.

***

"Something's off." Ferguson said when Hassim joined him. "Looks to me like the killer beat the victim to death. That's more than a single blow."

"Maybe they're escalating." Hassim said.

"Possibly, we'll have to get the autopsy done as soon as possible. I have a bad feeling we're dealing with a copy-cat."

"That's all we need is two of them out there." Hassim shone her light on the scene. "The witness who called it in was Molly. She's all right, shock's hitting her hard. They took her up to RIH."

"What was she doing her in the middle of the night?"

"She didn't say. The only thing I got from her was the killer took her phone."

"Wonderful." Ferguson stood up. "We'll hope it locked down before the killer picked it up, but we assume they have Molly's address and workplace."

"Her workplace is half the city." Hassim said and walked away from the scene. Ferguson followed her.

"Did they block off the other end of the alley?"

"Not immediately." Hassim said. "It took a few minutes for them to twig that it could be a murder scene."

"Damn." Ferguson took a deep breath. "She's safe enough for the moment, let's deal with the scene, then talk to her. Give her a chance to get herself together."

They waited for the Scene of Crime team to arrive and record the murder scene. Hassim looked up Blue's number and gave him a heads up.

"Blue is headed up to the RIH in a taxi." She reported to Ferguson. "He knows not to talk to her about the incident until we get there."

He nodded but stared at the brick wall. Had he put Molly in harm's way? Was this a coincidence or something more worrying?

***

He watched the coat float downstream, the bar already sunk to the bottom. A weight should have lifted off his shoulders, but he felt no different. No matter what he pretended he'd always be a killer. Lady Macbeth's 'out damned spot' line made a lot more sense to him now.

Whatever, this part of his life was done, and he'd have to move on. He walked back to the car and drove away.

At home he went on the computer to relax. He watched a movie, then another, but his mind wouldn't let him be. Then a breaking story popped up on his news feed.

'Another homeless person died tonight in an alley off 7th Ave tonight. Police haven't confirmed if this case is connected to the rash of killings in the past week.'

Cold travelled down his back. He was done, who had taken his place? How dare they? The first thing he thought was to call the police and tell them it wasn't him, but that was ridiculous. They'd arrest him, then his family would suffer. He couldn't do that.

He'd have to figure out how to stop them.

Somehow.

No one else could be the hand of fate, not while he was alive.

# CHAPTER 17
## Wednesday December 1

Molly hadn't been able to tell Ferguson any more than she had the first cop. She heard moaning, then footsteps. A light had shone on her face, and she was sure the killer said that they knew her. They stole her cellphone, which hadn't turned up at the scene according to Ferguson.

Blue had come and she cried on his shoulder for a while, but that didn't help the real problem. She'd run away from Tad. He'd said he loved her, and she ran away. What a coward. He deserved better than that. She didn't think she loved him. Not in the rom-com way of things. She didn't think of him constantly or dream about him. Now he'd probably never talk to her again. In a movie some crazy thing would bring them together again and it would be perfect.

She didn't live in a movie; if she did it sure as hell wasn't a rom-com.

Molly stared at the walls of her room. The doctors released her saying she'd strained her wrist and ankle, and should take it easy for a few days.

Some maniac killer had her phone, they'd recognized her. Was it someone she knew? Molly took a long shower, but it didn't slow the thoughts in her mind. She tried to tell herself that the murder had put her in shock. That was a lie. She was afraid of Tad. His vision of her was wrong. It had to be.

"Molly." Blue knocked on her door. "Phone for you." He stuck his hand through the crack between the door and the wall. She pushed herself off her bed and took the phone.

"Hello?"

"Molly are you okay? I saw the news and your phone went straight to voice mail. I called Blue because I had to know you were all right."

"I'm sorry I ruined the evening." Molly choked on the words.

"Ruined the evening?" Tad paused for a few breaths. "That was all me. I didn't mean to dump everything on you like that. I don't blame you for running away from me."

"You don't?" Molly clutched the phone.

"I'm not upset about it." Tad lowered his voice. "I've never said I loved anyone before. I'm not surprised I messed it up."

Molly laughed then couldn't stop. She imagined Tad on the other end of the line wondering about this crazy woman, then hanging up. Only he didn't. He started to laugh with her. It started with a bitter edge to it but morphed into something more authentic.

"I'm sorry," Molly hiccoughed and giggled. "It just struck me that neither of us have a clue."

"That's the truth." Tad said. "I'm glad you're okay."

"Thanks." Molly said. "Let's have dinner tomorrow after work. Do you like McDonalds, Wendy's or A&W?"

"A&W for sure." He sounded like she asked him to the finest place in town."

"How about you pick me up at nine and we'll go there and talk." Exhaustion hit Molly like a wall. "Gotta go. Bye."

"Bye, I—" His words were cut off as Molly hung up and rolled over on her bed. She should really take Blue's phone back to him, but her body refused to move.

***

The newest victim's autopsy was bumped to the head of the line. Ferguson sat at his desk absorbing the findings. The weapon was different. Thicker and lighter. There had been multiple blows both pre and post mortem, most of them to the shoulders and back.

He tried to imagine the scene. The killer comes across the victim and begins beating him. The victim fights back and takes a solid blow to the head, goes down and the killer finishes the job. They hear Molly and shine a flashlight at her. Did they come to the end of the alley to finish off the witness? That didn't make sense. She'd fled out of sight. It would be stupid to chase her through the streets.

That suggested they wanted the phone. They knew who she was. If the phone wasn't locked before they picked it up, they would have everything about Molly's life. Her home, her work, her friends.

He'd told Molly in no uncertain terms she was to go nowhere alone, or out at all at night. She looked scared enough to listen. A cruiser would drive by her apartment occasionally, as part of their shift. They were to take note of license plates of cars parked within sight of the front doors. He didn't expect much to come from that, but given her history, it was the most sensible thing to do.

"Hey Ferguson." Hassim put a coffee on his desk. "Anything interesting in the autopsy?"

"Unless the killer had a complete break, it isn't the same person. Nothing matches up."

"Heard a couple of the guys talking about an early morning call. Someone reported a body in the river. They went and fetched it only to find a black coat. It had been sliced open. Somebody came within a finger's breadth of losing their guts."

"And you are telling me this because?" Ferguson picked up his cup and sipped at the coffee.

Hassim put a sheet of paper on his desk. "You might have missed this with all the ruckus last night. The Scene of Crime people from the attack Monday morning."

Ferguson picked it up and read it. "They found down at the scene?"

"It was stuck on some blood on the victim. Maybe she'd been swinging that machete around."

"The coat this morning was a down coat?"

"Got it in one. It's with the lab now. Might be a long shot, but that could be our killer's coat."

"This is more than a curiousity." Ferguson leaned back and eyed Hassim through the steam from his cup.

"It's a high-end coat. Only one shop in town is authorized to sell it."

"If we get a list of buyers, it could narrow the field, but how many years back do we need to go?"

"One of the lab techs is a winter coat geek. She said every year this coat is slightly different. She's researching the year now."

"Let me know as soon as you have word." Ferguson grinned. "And we'll pay that store a visit."

"Another thing." Hassim handed him another paper. "This just came through, got a match on the victim's prints. The vic just go out of jail for fighting with a security guard at the storage shelter."

"Do we have a photo of the guard?"

"They made the front page." Hassim dropped a final sheet of paper on the desk. "The guard got fired for using excessive force a month or two back."

"Why does this guy look familiar?"

"I wondered that too. Then I thought about O'Brian and his buddies." She held up her phone with a video paused. It showed O'Brian holding Molly's coat, and behind them the man from the front-page photo. "That would be the third of our pathetic trio."

"A little pay back?" Ferguson held the phone and the photo together. "Maybe he thought he'd deal with the guy who got him in trouble. What's his real name?"

"Sam Willis, same name as the guy who owns the security company, but no relation. His co-workers said in the article he liked to play up the name to push people around."

"I wonder if the boss Willis remembers Sam?" Ferguson put his cup down. "I'll phone and see if he's free to talk to us."

It took him the better part of an hour to reach Henry Willis' executive assistant.

"I will give Mr. Willis your message."

"Thanks." Ferguson hung up. "Talk about being hard to reach."

"No kidding." Hassim looked up from her phone. "Though I'm not surprised. He's a wheeler dealer but likes to keep his name out of the news. He makes a pile of money but doesn't make a splash like others do giving it away. He lives in a monstrous pile of brick in Bachelor Heights. His son Henry Thaddeus Willis has a condo in Aberdeen area."

Ferguson flipped back through his notebook. "I thought so. The guy who was at the coffee shop with Molly when Colm harassed her is named Tad Willis. Wonder if there's a connection?"

"He was a bit of a handful a few years back, but nothing criminal. Dropped out of the public eye a couple of years back." Hassim waved her phone.

"The internet is scary." She held up the phone with a picture on it.

"Looks like the same guy." Ferguson checked his notes. "I'll check with Constable Post. He did the interview about the coffee shop incident."

***

Hassim parked in front of the 'Expeditions' store. Ferguson was going to try to track down Molly's friend. She figured the easiest thing was to ask Molly, but Ferguson didn't want to get her involved in that part of the investigation. Maybe he worried she'd call and warn him.

Either way it wasn't her problem. Hassim walked into the store and looked for a salesperson. She didn't see any, but she did see a rack of coats for 50% off. None of them looked like the one in her photo. She saw a couple she would have liked for herself, but even at half-price they were twice as much as she'd ever spent on a coat. Maybe the killer was more than comfortable middle class. But what would set off someone wealthy enough to wear that coat to kill, then discard it in the river? The only thing she could think of was money. Killing the homeless wouldn't make anyone richer. Did a homeless person cost someone a lot of money?

Pathi Bajwa was wealthy, and his family would stay wealthy. She'd checked out the children as a pro forma part of the investigation into Bajwa's death. Perhaps they deserved another look from a different direction.

"Excuse me, may I help you?" A man in his forties dressed in cargo pants and a plaid shirt that could have been tailored to fit him.

"Yes, I'm looking for this coat." She showed him the photo on her phone.

"Sorry. They are out of stock." He didn't look sorry.

"Out of stock?" Hassim lifted her brows. "How many do you carry?"

"Those coats are special order." The man already looked tired of the conversation.

"So you have a list of people who ordered the coat?" Hassim smiled. Things were looking up.

"That list would be confidential." He frowned and stepped away.

Hassim took out her badge and showed him. It didn't make him any happier. "The coat in this photo may be involved in a murder case." She handed him the phone.

"The owner was killed?" The man paled. "That is quite a cut in the front."

"The owner wasn't killed." Hassim put her badge away. "We found it in the river. No body."

"That's a relief." He handed her the phone. "Sorry, I couldn't help you."

"We haven't finished our conversation yet." Hassim smiled at him. "Tell me more about these coats."

"They are made to the client's measurements and preferences. The coat can be purchased in any colour, some may have battery operated heating elements in them. Just for the pockets or for the entire torso."

"This coat didn't have any heating elements." Hassim took her phone back and put it away.

"No, it wouldn't." The man looked horrified. "The owner was a purist and trusted our unique down to do its work."

"Was?" Hassim's heart sank.

"Yes, sadly the buyer died just after he picked up his coat. That would be in October of last year."

"What happened to the coat?"

"I wouldn't know, you'd need to ask the family."

"I will need to know the name of the family."

"The list is protected by confidentiality." The man said and turned away.

"I could phone every family who had a male member die and ask them about the coat. Of course, I would have to explain why." Hassim grinned and the man froze.

"That is blackmail."

"That is police work."

He turned to face her, shaking so much she worried he might attack her. "Come with me." He led her behind the counter and typed furiously on the computer. A moment later he hit print and handed her the paper. Since he didn't say anything more, Hassim took the paper and glanced at the name. Munson.

"Don't recognize the name."

"Not all wealthy people wish to advertise the fact." The man almost snarled at her. "They do all value their privacy."

"I will be discreet." Hassim folded the sheet and put it in her notebook. "Thank you for your cooperation."

"If you are done, I have work to do."

Hassim nodded and left. Probably just as well she'd never need to buy anything from the place. When she sat in the car, she looked at the paper again. It listed the man's name, but no address. She couldn't even be sure if the man was from Kamloops.

"Good thing there is the internet," she told herself and started the car.

***

Ferguson called the number Tad Willis had given to Constable Post. It was picked up almost immediately.

"Tad here."

"Sergeant Ferguson. I have a few questions for you."

"Ferguson, weren't you the one who saved Molly's life last year?"

"You could put it that way." Ferguson remembered the blonde's face as she died. He did his job, but it wasn't something he celebrated.

"Look, I'm in the middle of prepping for supper. Can you come by The Loop at four? I should be able to take a break then."

"The Loop?" Ferguson couldn't disguise the surprise in his voice.

"Yeah, I cook there most days. Sometimes I help out at the Café."

"I will see you at four then." Ferguson hung up and shook his head. What was the heir to the Willis fortune doing working as a cook in The Loop? He'd find out soon enough. His phone said it was one-thirty. He needed to have some lunch. He squashed the temptation to go to the Loop and try out Willis' cooking. Instead, he texted Hassim to meet him at The Noble Pig. Her text came back saying she be there in a few minutes.

Ferguson let dispatch know where he was going and headed out. He regretted the decision to walk almost immediately. The wind howled along Victoria, but it would be just as fast to finish the walk as it would be to return and take his car.

The host showed him to a table in the corner and left him with a menu. Ferguson sipped at his second cup of coffee as Hassim walked in and came over to him.

"I scored a mixed bag with the coat." She hung her coat on the hook, then filled him in on what she'd learned. "After lunch I hit the computer and get the background on Munson. All I know so far is that he had a really expensive taste in coats."

"That's a good start. I agree with looking at who may have lost money on Bajwa's death, but it will be hard to dig much up."

"I don't expect to find much. Most of what he had was shares in businesses and projects. Those shares won't vanish on his death. It will be inconvenient to make any changes in those shares until the will probates. That could take a year or more."

"Perhaps someone's on a tight timeline." Ferguson held up a finger as the server came to take their orders.

"Could be," Hassim continued when the server had left. "But I find it hard to imagine that any of those projects would be set on such a tight schedule. Maybe a change in circumstance, but the people we're looking at could loose half their money and still have more money than we'll make in a lifetime."

"As true as that may be, it could be a pride thing."

"I'll know better once I get into the research. Did Willis get back to you?"

"Not yet," Ferguson grimaced. "I may have to ask the higher ups to do what they can. But on a side note, Tad Willis volunteers at The Loop. Probably how he met Molly."

"Makes sense. Do we know if he is Henry Thaddeus yet?"

"I'm meeting him at four at The Loop. He didn't seem at all worried that the police wanted to talk to him."

"Probably thinking you're following up on the incident with Colm."

"Maybe." Ferguson drank some water. "I'll find out soon enough."

***

It surprised Molly when Ferguson buzzed to get access to the apartment. She let him and briefly thought about changing her clothes but didn't have the energy. He'd have to deal with the sweatpants and t-shirt.

"How are you doing?"

"Sore, mad at myself," Molly dropped on the couch and waved Ferguson to a chair. "I broke a promise and ended up in trouble."

"Promise?"

"Yeah, I promised an aunt that I wouldn't walk by myself at night. I'd call her, or a taxi, instead I stormed off to take the bus."

"Don't be too hard on yourself. We all make stupid choices." Ferguson chuckled. "You're lucky it only cost you a cell phone."

"Don't remind me." Molly sighed. "I tried the track your phone app this morning. Nothing, like it didn't exist."

"Probably destroyed it because of that kind of app."

"At least all the important information was backed up, but it's a nuisance not having a phone."

"Maybe Tad will take you shopping for a new one."

"How did you...Oh right, the mess at the coffee shop. Of course, you'd have read the report." Molly rubbed her temples. "I feel like I'm working with only half a brain today."

"Not an uncommon reaction to trauma like last night."

"Tell me about it." Molly put a hand to her mouth at the bitterness of her tone.

"I've had to meet with the psychiatrist more than once." Ferguson answered. "This kind of work does things to you. It's important to keep up the maintenance."

"I know, but I don't have a therapist I can trust with all the stuff that's going on with this case. It's bringing up a shitload of bad memories." Molly pulled up her legs and hugged her knees.

"You've done a lot for us. If you need to stop, just say the word."

"I don't think I can stop. I have to work through it." Molly pushed back tears. "It will haunt me either way."

"I understand." Ferguson paused and gazed at her until she her face burned. "I will try to connect you with a therapist who specializes in working with peace officers."

"I'd appreciate that."

Ferguson laughed. "Wait until you've had a couple of sessions, then thank me if you still want to."

"They're that good, are they?"

"One of the best," Ferguson said. "You won't need to hold anything back."

"Good." Molly smiled. "I will look forward to talking to them."

"His name is Giles Dellacourt. He'll email you if he can fit you in." Ferguson's phone rang. "Ferguson here."

"Hello, I hear you wanted to talk to me." The voice was controlled and uncommitted. Molly could hear him from where she sat. "This is Henry Willis."

"Yes, just a couple of simple questions." Ferguson put his finger to his lips and Molly nodded.

"Good, I don't have time to waste."

"A man named Sam Willis was fired from a security company you own. I wondered if you remembered him, given your shared name."

"I remember tearing a strip off the person who hired him. I was unfortunate enough to have him do security for an event I put on. If ever there was a wannabe tough guy it was him. The incident with that homeless person gave me the excuse I needed."

"If it is possible to get his last known address, I would appreciate it."

"My executive assistant will call you. If you are done, I have work to do." He hung up. Ferguson stared at the phone for a few seconds, then shrugged and put it in his pocket.

"At least I got my answers before he hung up." Ferguson stood. "I have an appointment shortly. I'm glad you are holding together."

"Just barely." Molly got up, "but thanks for stopping by." She showed him out the door, then went to have a shower and change. Sweatpants just wouldn't do for Tad.

***

Ferguson sat across from Tad Willis and was surprised at the lack of spoiled rich kid vibes. Tad sat and talked to people around him for a few minutes.

"There's an office we can use." Tad led the way to what was more an oversized broom closet than office, but it had two chairs in it.

Ferguson took one and readied his notebook. "You are Henry Thaddeus Willis?"

"I don't use that name anymore. Call me Tad."

"Right. Tad." Ferguson got Tad's birthdate and address. Then continued the questioning. "You know Molly Callister?"

"I do." Tad shifted slightly in his chair and reddened. "I'd like to know her better."

"Tell me about two weeks ago Tuesday."

"The coffee shop." Tad nodded. "A guy came in looking for a fight. I would have given it to him, but Molly stopped me and talked him out of it."

"There was a knife involved?"

"The guy took a knife out, but fumbled it trying to open it. Molly covered it with her foot, then convinced him it was outside. The guy was drunk enough to buy it. He left and we didn't see him again. I talked to Constable Post about it."

"Yesterday, you and Molly went out for dinner and a movie."

"Yeah, we'd argued, and I wanted to make it up to her. Actually, I was a doofus and I was celebrating her giving me a second chance."

"Molly ended up walking to the Lansdown Exchange by herself. Did you have another fight?"

"Not so much a fight as me being an idiot and dumping too much on her all at once. She panicked and almost ran out the door. I thought about following her, but she'd just get mad at me, so I went home."

"You heard that Molly is a witness to a murder that evening?"

"I did." Tad reddened. "I called her to ask if she was okay. She arranged to meet me at A&W for hamburgers."

"Do you know anyone who would want to hurt Molly?"

"Not really. Molly can rub some people the wrong way, but I can't imagine someone wanting to hurt her."

"The killer stated that he recognized Molly." Do you have any idea who that might be?"

"No, she keeps ending up in the news. I'm sure a lot of people know her from that. Not to mention the people she works with."

"You think any of them could be a danger to Molly?"

"From what I've heard they adore her."

"Tell me about the bruises on your face." Ferguson glanced up at him.

"I got drunk and lost a fight in a bar the weekend after we had our argument. I can give you the name of the place and you can confirm it."

Ferguson took down the details then left Tad to get back to work. He stopped in at the bar on the way to the station and confirmed Tad's story. Back at the station he wrote up the interview and waited for Hassim to join him. He fetched a coffee to give him something to do.

She came over to the desk as he worked on the backlog of paperwork.

Ferguson drank the now cold coffee as Hassim filled him in one what she'd learned.

"Charles Munson's parents died in a car crash. Witnesses said they'd swerved to avoid a man pushing a cart across the street. He has good reason to hate the homeless. When Bajwa died at the hands of a street person, he must have cracked and declared war. Munson has an i3 BMW electric and a Mercedes, both black.

"So he starts killing, just like that?" Ferguson pushed the half empty cup away.

"Maybe Molly is right and the first two were more or less accidents, but getting away with them he gets bolder and goes hunting."

"This is all speculation until we have enough evidence to make a case." Ferguson shook his head.

"Munson doesn't know that." Hassim leaned on the desk. "How about we go and ask him about that coat? He might crack."

"Not likely." Ferguson sighed. "But it isn't like we have anything better to do. At least we have the unmarked car back, so we can be discreet." He stood up and Hassim followed him down the parking lot.

Rain started falling as they wound up to Aberdeen. Even with the wipers on it was hard to see. They passed the house twice before finding it. No lights were on, and the garage door was open.

"Let's knock and see what's what." Hassim got out of the car and Ferguson followed her.

"I don't like this." He took out his torch and shone it ahead of them. He flashed it over the garage as they stepped from the driveway to the walk up to the front door. "Hold on."

Hassim stopped and turned her flashlight on. "What do you see?"

"What is that spot on an otherwise spotless garage floor?"

"Oil maybe?" Hassim stepped up beside him and shone her light around. "There are a couple of other spots."

"Wrong place for an oil leak." Ferguson looked at her. "And there is a charging station on the wall. The door is wide open, it is in open sight."

"Go for it." Hassim said. "I'll watch for trouble."

Ferguson crept into the garage and knelt beside the largest spot, peering at it closely. "Definitely not oil. It is the right colour for old blood."

"He's gone hunting." Hassim said. "I'll call it in and get someone to watch the house in case he returns."

"Call in a BOLO on the i3, extra eyes on Schubert St. and around Riverside Park. Anyone sees those plates, they call in immediately." Ferguson headed back to the car.

"Where are we going?" Hassim closed her door.

"We'll check downtown while the cruisers check Schubert and the park." He put the car in gear. "Who knows, we may get lucky."

# CHAPTER 18

Tad didn't talk to his father much anymore. His mother had left him all her money with just enough going to his father to keep him from challenging the will. Since then, every girl he'd dated had assumed that access to his money came as part of the bargain.

Working as a volunteer cook for a community program was as far as he could get from the money-based life of his father and the people like him.

Molly sent confusing emotions through Tad. She didn't seem to care about the money. She knew now that he was rich, but she still paid for the refreshments while he paid for the movie. He couldn't imagine her settling for being the mistress. It would be too much like a reversion to her earlier life.

She wanted him to be a friend. He wasn't sure what that meant. Had he ever had a true friend?

Tad shook himself. He'd better get a move on, or he'd be late. Disappointing Molly had become very high on his list of things to avoid. Rain made the dark blacker. He picked up his umbrella then locking the door behind him, Tad climbed into the car and started it up.

His mind was already on Molly as he backed out of the driveway. He drove down the hill to her apartment. A route he could drive in his sleep. Once driving past her building was enough to calm him.

He'd stopped the habit, thinking she would be mad at him for intruding on her life.

When he parked in front of her apartment, he texted her and waited at the door to walk her to the car. His heart skipped when she took his arm. It wasn't much of a drive to the A&W on 8th Street, but there was a special warmth to having her in the passenger seat. He fought the silly grin that wanted to take over his face.

He parked beside the restaurant and walked in holding Molly's hand.

"What do you want?" Molly asked. "I'm buying tonight."

"An Uncle Burger combo, bacon and cheese with root beer." Tad squashed the impulse to insist on paying. "I'll find a table after I've used the washroom."

She squeezed his hand, then let him go.

Someone came in the door as he rounded the corner and bumped into him.

"Sorry, oh hi Tad long time no see." The person smiled at him.

"Hello Peter, what can I do for you?" Tad kept his face neutral. It wasn't Peter's fault that Tad was coming to loathe his money.

"Come with me." Peter pulled a pistol out of his pocket for Tad to see. "And no one else gets hurt."

Tad forced himself not to turn and look at Molly. He held his hands out.

"I don't know what you want, but you have my attention."

"Outside and we'll get into your car." Peter pushed him through the door. "Give me your keys."

Tad swallowed and handed the keys to Peter. He remembered Peter as being very intense. No way Tad was going to risk angering him.

"In the car, the driver's seat, put your hands on the steering wheel." Peter unlocked the door.

Tad climbed in and did as he was told. It was too late to argue. Peter hand cuffed his hands to the wheel, then put a zip tie around Tad's neck and the head rest. He put his finger to his lips, then walked around to the passenger door and climbed in carefully fastening his seat belt with one hand while keeping the gun on Tad with the other.

"In case you get any heroic notions, I have a seat belt and you don't. Crash the car and you'll snap your neck."

Tad nodded. Peter pushed the button to start the car and put the car in reverse. Tad backed up and Peter switched to drive.

"Pioneer Park." Peter kept the gun pointed at Tad. "You're going to help me have a discussion with your father."

Numbly Tad drove through the downtown and onto River St. When he got to the parking lot, Peter told him to drive on the walking path under the Red Bridge. Peter ordered him to stop and put the car in park.

"Which pocket is your cell phone?"

"Inside left." Tad stared into the dark and tried to stop the shaking in his hands. He wasn't going to get out of this alive. *Sorry, Molly.*

Peter took the phone and used Tad's face to open it.

"Listing your father as Henry Willis. That's cold." Peter dialed the number. "Hello Mr. Willis. I would like to talk business with you. Don't hang up or your son will regret it."

Tad closed his eyes and tried to imagine his father caring enough about Tad to stay on the line. One of his father's nephews was almost a perfect replacement for Tad. Henry Willis might be happy to be rid of his rebellious son.

"He's alive for the moment, but his remaining so depends on you." Peter's face was lit by the faint light of the phone and his face scared Tad more than the gun. Peter might have been ordering pizza for all the emotion he showed.

"Here's what you do. Keep the phone on. If you lose the connection, you kill your son. You try texting anyone, it will delay you. The distance between your house and my location is about a ten minute drive. You will keep up a running commentary of where you are. If you take too long, your son is dead. Go straight to your car. I'm counting the seconds. Don't waste time."

"Start your car and take Halston to Hwy 5 turn south." Tad's father spoke about where he was driving, occasionally interrupted by Peter to give directions.

"Park your car and bring your phone with you. Put the flashlight on so I can see you. Keep walking until you see the lights of the car." Peter checked the gun then got out of the car. "I'll be back in a few minutes."

He vanished immediately into the darkness.

Tad couldn't see anything in the rear-view mirror. He tried to twist his hand to honk the horn, but couldn't bend down because of the zip tie.

A shot sounded, then another, then he couldn't count fast enough to keep up. He hung his head and closed his eyes. Tears leaked through them. He didn't get along with his father, but that didn't mean he wanted him dead. Being dead would mean his father would never understand him.

***

Molly picked up their meal and looked for Tad. He wasn't anywhere in the restaurant. Maybe he had to wait in the washroom. She found a seat and waited. When he still didn't show up, she went to the counter and asked one of the people to check the men's washroom. They came back quickly to say there was no one there.

She looked around and saw that Tad's car was gone. Something was badly wrong.

"Hi Molly." A man she recognized from the altercation on the street the week before smiled at her, and her stomach turned to jelly. "Don't make a fuss and come with me if you want to see your boyfriend again."

Molly turned toward the counter, but the man put a hand on her elbow and squeezed.

"Now." He pushed her outside and forced her hands behind her. A zip tie cut into her wrists. He threw her into the passenger seat of a large black truck, fastened the seatbelt, then ran around and jumped in the driver's side. Tires slid on the wet pavement as he raced out of the parking lot.

"Do you remember me?" The man leered at her. "You should, I gave you the best ride of your life."

Molly's stomach rebelled and she almost puked as the man began reciting a detailed memory of what he'd done to her body. "I saw you from the alley and knew immediately who you were. Figured I would give you one last thrill."

She should have expected someday to run into a past client, but it had never occurred to her. Leaving the life meant moving forward toward the future. He knew what had happened to Tad. The thought of never seeing him again brought tears to her eyes.

"Don't worry." The man reached over and patted her thigh. "You'll be with him again soon." He laughed and Molly shuddered.

They wove through the evening traffic as he talked about what he was going to do, before and after he killed her. Gradually her fear gave way to a cold anger. She hadn't survived only to die whimpering at the hands of this poor imitation of a human being. Plans formed in her mind. This asshole would regret grabbing her. She'd die making sure of that.

***

"Respond to 8th and Fortune. Possible abduction reported at the A&W." Dispatch announced.

"Dispatch we're on our way." Ferguson replied and turned the car around and headed to Fortune. They pulled in the lot and Ferguson was out of the car almost before it stopped.

"You reported a possible abduction?" He leaned on the counter.

"That'd be Mary." The boy called her over. "Describe what you saw."

"There was this woman, her boyfriend vanished, then this other guy came in and talked to her. They left together, but she didn't look happy." She pointed at a table with food sitting on it. "They left without even touching their food."

"Any idea of the vehicle they left in?"

"All I saw was a big black truck. It might have been a Ford." Mary's hands shook. "I should have done something to stop him."

"You did the right thing to call us." Hassim said.

"The license plate may have ended with 2043." A boy came up beside Mary. "I was delivering a meal to a car in the lot and a big truck took off way too fast. I could only get the last four numbers."

Ferguson yanked out his phone and called dispatch. "Watch for a large black pickup, possibly a Ford, last four digits on the plate 2043."

"We'll get the word out."

Ferguson pulled up a picture on his phone. "Is this the girl?"

"Yeah," Mary said. "That's her."

"I'll need access to the video for the past hour."

"I'll get the manager." The boy ran to the back and came back a with a minute with a slightly older boy in tow, his name tag read 'Alan Assistant Manager'.

"Access to your video." Ferguson held out his badge.

"It will be in the manager's office." Alan led Ferguson to the back and unlocked the door. "I could get fired for this." He sat at the computer and rewound the footage from the cameras.

"There. That's her. Go forward in real time." Ferguson watched Molly walk back and forth, pick up her order and walk to the table. She sat for a while then returned to the counter.

"She asked us to check the men's washroom." Alan said. "It was empty."

Molly headed back to the table, but a man stepped up beside her, a ballcap pulled low over his eyes.

"Print that." Ferguson ordered. Seconds later he held a few grainy photographs of Molly and the man.

Back out front Hassim was talking on the phone. "Right, thanks." She looked up at Ferguson. "Truck's registered to Sam Willis."

"If you were abducting someone, where would you take her?" Ferguson asked.

"Somewhere dark without a lot of people." Hassim shook her head. "Any alley in the city."

"Not good enough." Ferguson banged his leg with his fist. A cruiser pulled up by the restaurant with the lights going. A uniformed officer got out and came into the store.

"Attention." Ferguson spoke loudly enough to turn every head in the place toward him. "This officer is going to ask you a few questions. Do not leave until she or I have spoken to you."

Two more cruisers arrived, and more officers came into the restaurant.

Ferguson gave the printouts to the first uniformed officer and pointed to it. "See if anyone noticed anything. One officer on each door." He held up his badge. The constables took their places.

Ferguson started on one side of the room and the constable on the other. An older man put his hand up and Ferguson walked over to him.

"The man called her by name. Said something about her boyfriend."

Ferguson took out his notebook. "Let's start with your name and birthdate."

It didn't take long to work through the small crowd in the room. Most people denied seeing anything. As they gave their statements they were allowed to leave.

"Ferguson." Hassim shouted from the counter. "Report of shots fired in the park near the Red Bridge."

"Let's go." He ran out to the car and started it up as Hassim jumped in. They headed for the downtown.

Ferguson carefully drove the speed limit to the parking lot at Pioneer Park. A single car sat in the lot, accompanied by a half dozen cruisers. Rain poured down so Ferguson got their rain gear from the trunk. Then walked up to a sergeant holding a clipboard in a plastic bag and was directing the other officers.

"What do we have?" Ferguson asked.

"The car is registered to Henry Willis. Officers are searching the park now. The rain is making things difficult."

"You're doing the work that needs to be done. Keep it up."

"Need an ambulance at Pioneer Park." The sergeant's radio crackled. "Two people with gun shot wounds. We're widening the search."

Ferguson turned his flashlight on. "I'm going to have a look at the scene before the rain washes everything away." The Sergeant nodded and made a note.

The flashlight did little to illuminate the night. The lights on the bridge weren't much better. The men lay groaning on the soaked grass as an officer gave first aid. Another constable put two guns in separate bags and wrote a notation on a tag. She noticed Ferguson watching her.

"Since they are alive, I wanted to get the guns out of the picture."

"Good thinking, have they been searched for other weapons?"

"They were searched while their injuries were being assessed. No other weapons were found. Officers are searching for a possible third suspect."

Ferguson nodded. "I doubt they arrived in the same car. Where's the other one?"

"They're looking for that too."

The radio crackled. "We've found a car with a person secured inside. The doors aren't locked. The man is alive, but appears to be in shock."

"I'll be right there." Ferguson walked over to where two constables held flashlights on the car. A third was unlocking a set of hand cuffs. A cut zip tie lay on the ground.

Tad stumbled out of the car, a red mark on his throat and more on his wrists. "How is my father? Are they both dead?"

"They're both alive." Ferguson told him. "Aiming a gun in the daylight is hard enough, never mind the dark. They're lucky."

He caught Tad as his knees gave way and lowered him to the ground.

"Ambulances have arrived." The radio squawked.

"Can you walk, or do you want to wait for a stretcher?" Ferguson asked.

"I'll walk, just give me a minute."

A constable opened a plastic poncho and helped Tad put it on.

More powerful lights arrived on the scene and showed paramedics moving the men onto stretchers then carrying them to where the gurneys waited under the bridge. Faint shouting came through the rain.

"If they're shouting at each other, they should be fine." The constable put a hand on Tad's shoulder.

"I'm ready." Tad climbed to his feet and walked toward the bridge. Ferguson stayed beside him as the other officers secured the car.

"I want to ride with my father." Tad said.

"Don't see why not." The water on the ground had soaked through Ferguson's boots.

"Molly." Tad stopped walking. "How's Molly? she must hate me."

"She reported you missing." Ferguson put a hand on Tad's elbow and got him moving again. "She's not mad at you."

Tad sighed as he reached the ambulance and climbed in. The doors shut cutting off what Tad was saying to his father and the ambulance headed off.

"You didn't tell him about Molly." Hassim frowned.

"I didn't want to break him." Ferguson watched the other ambulance follow the first. "He wouldn't have gone if he knew she was missing."

"You're probably right."

Ferguson scrubbed the rain off his face. "We have work to do."

***

Charles parked by the Sandman Centre and walked into the dark rain, holding a crowbar in his right hand. The rain didn't bother him much. He had his old waterproof parka. With the hood up he was warm everywhere but the hand holding the crowbar. When he reached the Rivers Trail he mentally flipped a coin then headed west along the path.  Even the street people would be holed up somewhere in this weather. Maybe he'd spot someone, maybe he wouldn't. Maybe he'd kill, maybe he wouldn't. The desire burned in him, but he tried to focus on his target; the one who'd usurped his vengeance.

He didn't have any plan of how to find the interloper, but wandered through the night letting fate guide him.

***

Molly's abductor parked near the tennis courts. He pulled her out of the truck and put an arm around her shoulder.

"We see anyone, we're just a couple out for a walk. You don't want anyone else to get hurt, do you?"

Molly bit her cheek and nodded. He forced her to walk toward the river.

"You know the advantage of working security?" The man spoke casually. "You get to know all the hidey holes. It will be days before they find you."

Molly's knees quivered, but she refused to give in to fear. When she didn't say anything, he tightened his grip on her shoulder.

"You aren't much fun." The man growled. "You want to live longer, you're going to give me everything I want."

"Now that's incentive." Molly's voice burst the bonds she'd laid on it. "Die now, or die later after you've raped me."

"Nah, you can't rape a hooker." He laughed. "You want it, however you can get it. You are going to die happy."

They crossed the asphalt page.

"You want to know something?" The ice in Molly's gut exploded into heat. "You're pathetic. You all are. Buying sex because you're so afraid of women, it's the only way you can get it up. I'll guarantee every hooker you've fucked lay there wishing you'd just die while they played along to get your money."

He shouted something at her and punched her in the gut. Molly gasped for air, then his hands went around her neck, and he mashed his lips against hers, forcing his tongue into her mouth.

Molly bit down as hard as she could. He pushed her away and screamed. Somehow, she stayed on her feet. He was a blacker darkness. When he got close enough, she spat the thing in her mouth at his face, then kicked out with all her strength.

Her boot connected with his shin, and he bent over in pain. She kicked again, but this time he caught her foot and dumped her on the ground.

"You're going to die screaming in pain, bitch." The man's words didn't form properly with a chunk of his tongue missing.

Molly pulled her legs back ready to try one last time to cause the bastard pain.

"I found you." A man's voice said from the path. "You killed my prey."

"What?" The abductor said, before something thudded into him. The two wrestled in the dark as Molly tried to scramble back. The men cursed each other. They looked like a single beast writhing in rage. She couldn't get out of the way. The fighters stepped on her then fell down and over the bank still striking each other.

Someone knelt at her side and cut the zip tie from her wrist. Strong hands lifted her to her feet and faced her toward the lights of River St.

"Go quickly before one of them kills the other."

"Edwin?" Molly rasped.

"I couldn't leave you to the night." He shoved her and she had to run to catch her balance, and once she started, she couldn't stop. Not until she hit a tree and bounced to the ground. Dazed, Molly pushed herself to her feet and staggered on into the light and collapsed.

A cruiser drove past with the floodlight, she couldn't say how much later. The light made her wince and cover her face.

The car stopped and a police officer jumped out and ran to her.

"Hold on, help is coming." Then he chattered into his radio.

Molly's stomach twisted and she vomited on the sidewalk. The cop turned her on her side and stayed at her side as she emptied her stomach until all that was left was a hole inside her.

The paramedics arrived, wrapped her in a warm blanket and prepared to whisk her away to the hospital."

"Tad. Tad's missing." Molly clutched the officer's arm as she tried to get her mind to work. She had to give a description so they could look for him.

"Slow down." The cop put a hand over hers. "What was he wearing?"

"I can't think, I don't know." Molly wailed. "He drives a blue car."

"Last name?"

"Willis, Tad Willis.

"I'll let dispatch know and follow you to the hospital."

Molly tried to picture what Tad had been wearing. What colour was his coat, his pants? She lay on the gurney shivering.

The officer arrived right after the ambulance stopped at the Emergency entrance. "Tad has been located. He's here with his father. Now we need to take care of you. Tell me what you can about what happened?"

"This guy forced me into his truck and tied my hands. Then he forced me to walk into the park with him. He told me all the things he was going to do with me, then another guy jumped him. They fell down the hill fighting. Edwin came and made me run to the street."

"He was going to rape you, but was interrupted. Is that correct?"

"He tried to kiss me, and I bit him." Molly retched at the memory.

The paramedics helped onto the hospital bed enclosed by blue curtains a nurse took her blood pressure and temperature.

"If you need me, I'll be right there." The cop left through the gap in the curtain.

"Do you want to get out of those wet clothes?" The nurse helped her out of her clothes then gave her a blue gown and helped her put it on. Molly huddled under a blanket and thought about Tad. As long as she kept her mind on him, she didn't need to think about other things. The doctor came and went, then returned to tell her she was in shock and needed to rest.

"They told me Tad was here. Can I see him?"

"Tad?"

"Tad Willis, he came in with his father."

"I will ask the nurses."

He left her alone again. She shivered and thought about asking for another blanket.

"Molly." A nurse came in with a wheelchair. "Tad is in the surgery waiting room. I'll take you there." She pushed Molly through the halls as Molly tugged the blanket tighter around her.

***

Tad paced in the waiting room. The doctors had told him that gunshot wounds were serious, but his father's vitals were strong. He'd heard that before. When he was twelve and his mother went in for routine surgery. A doctor came out and talked to his father.

"Is mom going to be all right?" He'd asked.

"No." His father said. "You're going to have to be strong."

Strong meant not crying at the funeral. Strong meant keeping his face like stone just like his father.

Tad didn't want to be strong again.

A nurse pushed a woman in a wheelchair into the waiting room. She looked small and frail, huddled beneath a blanket.

"Tad." The woman said and he realized it was Molly.

"Molly." He ran over and knelt beside her. "I was so worried."

Molly's arms went around him and held him tight. He lifted her out of the chair and sat holding her on a chair in the waiting room. She sobbed in his arms as his cheeks ran with tears.

The nurse brought a blanket and wrapped it around them, then left them alone.

He didn't know how long it was before the doctor came out of the operating room.

"Your father did well. He's in recovery. A nurse will take you there."

Tad buried his face in Molly's hair. He didn't need to be strong, not today.

They sat in the recovery room until Tad's father opened his eyes. He looked around until he saw Tad, then sighed and smiled slightly.

"Good to see you, son."

"Thank you for coming for me." Tad's arms were full with a sleeping Molly so he couldn't wipe the tears from his face. His father didn't say anything but reached out a hand to take Tad's. If Tad didn't know better, he would have thought his father's eyes glistened.

# CHAPTER 19
## Thursday December 2

Ferguson worked on the enormous amounts of paperwork generator by the night's events. Even without needing to write up Tad's abduction and the shoot out, he still had Molly's experience and the two dead killers at the bottom of the hill.

His gut hurt, he thought it was guilt. Molly had enough trauma to deal with, she didn't need an abduction and attempted rape. His phone rang providing a welcome distraction.

"Ferguson."

"Giles Dellacourt. I got your message about taking in a civilian client. Since it was you, I thought I'd phone and talk to you instead of automatically refusing."

"I appreciate that." Ferguson picked up a pen to play with. "We had her working the homeless community during the killings this past week or so. It may have been foolish, but she agreed and did good work for us. We have IDs for all the victims because of her."

"Good for her, but that isn't enough to make an exception."

"It brought up old traumas, but she pushed through. Then a copy-cat killer grabbed her and tried to rape her. She fought free and escaped while the guy fought with another man, who we suspect was the spree killer."

"Still hard, but no go." Giles sighed. "It isn't that I'm not sympathetic, but the contract is very specific to sworn officers. There is a woman who used to be a cop, she works over video calls. I'll text you her number."

"Thanks." Ferguson rubbed his stomach. He'd expected this result, but he'd promised to try.

"And Ferguson." Giles said. "Let me know how it goes. She sounds like one tough woman."

"She is." Ferguson's phone beeped to let him know a text had arrived. He dialed the number.

"Nancy Watson. How can I help you?"

"Sergeant Ferguson from the Kamloops RCMP. I'm calling to find out if you are taking clients. Giles Dellacourt gave me your name."

"Yeah, I knew Giles back in the day. He was the one to inspire my change from cop to therapist. Tell me a bit more about this client."

Once again Ferguson went through the background to Molly needing the therapy. This time he mentioned the process of her getting clean and off the street.

"Ouch." Nancy said at the conclusion of Ferguson's story. "I hear stories like that and wonder how the people are alive, never mind functioning in society. I have a bit of space, but I'm not cheap and it sounds like she can't afford me."

"I'll pay the bill myself if I have to." Ferguson tossed the pen on his desk.

"I tell you what." Nancy paused. "I'm working on a book about multiple traumas in crime victims. If she allows me to use her as a case study, I can make a substantial cut to my normal rates."

"That would be fantastic." Ferguson pumped his fist. "I'll talk to her about it and get her to contact you. Her name is Molly Callister."

"You haven't talked to her about this?" Nancy sounded cold.

"I have." Ferguson said. "She asked for help finding a counsellor who wouldn't run screaming when she told her story."

"This isn't a romantic interest, is it?"

"She's the age of my oldest daughter. I want to make up for dragging her back into hell."

"Okay, if she calls me, I'll talk to her and take it from there."

"That's all I can ask." Ferguson leaned back and pumped his fist again.

"And sergeant." Nancy's voice warmed up. "You may want to seek help yourself about this."

"I'll talk to Giles." Ferguson promised and hung up.

"You look like the cat that ate the canary." Hassim sat in the chair facing the desk.

"If Molly's up for it, I've found a counsellor who will work with her. She's Giles' recommendation."

"You can let Molly know when we talk to her. She's given a bare bones statement, but wants to go over it in more detail with us."

"What about Willis and Bajwa?" Ferguson asked.

"We aren't on that case. Someone else is talking to them."

"That's good, we have enough to wrap up as it is."

"I've asked them to cc us on the write up of the interviews." Hassim said. "I heard that their lawyers were already talking to the crown and asking about a plea bargain."

"Must be nice to be rich." Ferguson stood and grabbed his coat. "Let's go chat with Molly."

***

Molly woke up curled in a recliner chair, blankets tucked in around her. She didn't recognize where she was, and her heart raced, then remembered what happened. Blue had brought her comfortable clothes, but since she didn't need to be admitted she'd stayed with Tad in his father's room. Blue sat in the other chair and smiled at her.

"Where's Tad?" Molly asked.

"He's giving his statement about last night." Blue frowned. "That had to be rough."

"That's for sure." Molly sat up and pulled the blanket around her. "I don't think he's ever had anything like that happen before."

"I doubt it." Blue stretched. "Mr. Willis is still sleeping, how about we go grab some food and wake up."

Molly got paper and pen from the nursing station and left a note for Tad. Then they headed for the cafeteria. Ferguson and Hassim got off the elevator they were going to take down.

"We're going to get some breakfast and coffee." Blue said. "You want to join us?"

"Why not?" Ferguson stepped back into the elevator and held the doors for them and Hassim.

The cafeteria wasn't very busy, so they found a table in the corner away from other people. Blue went to get breakfast for him and Molly.

"You doing okay?" Ferguson's smile came out a little twisted.

"He's been worrying non-stop about you." Hassim nudged him.

"I have a daughter your age." Ferguson leaned forward. "I get nightmares sometimes from the cases I work on."

"I'm not surprised." Molly nodded. "I would like to meet her sometime."

"She lives in Winnipeg and is a constable with their police force, but if she ever visits, I'll let you know."

"That would be cool." Molly shifted to get more comfortable in the chair. "I think I'm doing all right. I just woke up, so it is hard to tell, but I'm not shaking."

"You feel up to giving us a more detailed statement about last night?" Hassim took out a recorder. "It's fine if you want to wait a bit, but we'd like to clear the case off the books."

"I'll give it a try." Molly's stomach twinged, but she told it to shut up, and told the story from when she and Tad arrived at the A&W to when the cop found her on the street. Her hands shook uncontrollably while she talked, but neither Ferguson or Hassim made any comment or tried to rush her.

Blue returned with the food and put a plate in front of Molly along with a cup of coffee. He sat and ate his breakfast while Molly talked. She took a couple of sips of coffee, but couldn't touch the food until she was done, then she realized how hungry she was.

Hassim put the recorder away. "Thank you. I know how hard that had to be."

"Now that it's done, I'm surprised it wasn't harder." Molly picked up her fork and started on her breakfast.

Ferguson shook his head. "You never fail to amaze me. I don't think I would be so calm after that."

"Trauma is sneaky." Blue pushed his empty plate aside. "It doesn't always hit you how you expect it to."

Molly nodded and took another bite.

"Speaking of trauma." Ferguson slid a piece of paper across the table to her. "Nancy Watson is a cop turned therapist. She comes highly recommended."

"I think my benefits have a little coverage for therapy." Molly put the paper in her pocket "I will check and see."

"Nancy said she'd give a discount if you agreed to be a case study for her next book." Ferguson sighed. "I'm not sure what all is involved."

"I'll talk to her. Thanks." Molly returned to eating her breakfast.

"If the cost gets to be too much, let me know." Ferguson turned red and Hassim elbowed him again. Molly nodded. She didn't know what was going on, but it didn't matter at this moment.

"I will get the files to you tomorrow." Molly put her fork down. "I'd rather not have them in the apartment."

"Just drop them at the reception desk and let them know they're for me." Ferguson said. "We may not be in the building. We have other cases on the go."

"Okay." Molly felt a twinge. She wanted to wrap things up properly. "If you're off tomorrow evening, how about you drop by the apartment, and I'll cook supper. The social worker in me is demanding proper closure. Is there anything you can't eat."

"Not a thing." Hassim smiled. "I think we can make it work."

Ferguson glanced at her, then shrugged. "Sure, we'd be delighted. We'll be off about five. Thanks for all the help. You were an invaluable team member."

"Thanks." Molly looked down and her face heated. Ferguson and Hassim left. Molly got up to find Tad, then she spotted him across the cafeteria and walked over to meet him.

"How'd it go?" Molly took his hand.

"Not much fun, but I got through it." Tad smiled at her. "I could use something to eat."

"I'm over there." She pointed. "Grab what you want and come join us."

Tad joined her and Blue at the table. "That was nerve wracking. Even though I knew I was the victim, I kept thinking about what I was saying and would it get me into trouble."

"I know the feeling." Molly put a hand on his. "How are you doing with dealing with the events? It has to be hard, being kidnapped and thinking you're going to die and maybe your father with you."

"That's for sure. I'm sure there are nightmares in my future." Tad took a long breath, then started in on his meal.

Molly watched him, strangely comfortable with the silence.

"I need to get to work." Blue stood up. "I'll take a taxi down the hill. I'll see you this evening." He kissed the top of Molly's head then walked away.

"He's never done that before." Molly stared at Blue's back.

"How many times has he almost lost you?" Tad said. "That is got to be hard."

"I remember when I was sure I'd lost Blue." Molly shuddered. "I'll need to talk to him this evening."

"Let me know how it goes." Tad finished his meal then stared into space.

"What are you thinking?" Molly asked after almost a minute of silence.

"I don't like what money's done to my father." Tad looked her in the eyes. "I'm afraid that will be me someday. I'm seriously thinking of giving it all away and earning a living like a normal person."

"I don't know that I understand." Molly said. "You are you, and that won't change whether you have money or not."

"So you wouldn't mind?" Tad took her hand.

"It isn't up to me." Molly squeezed back. "Do what you need to do. But think it through first. If you had to work fulltime, you wouldn't be able to volunteer the same way at the Loop. I also wonder if giving it away is abdicating the responsibility."

"With great wealth comes great responsibility?" Tad grinned at her. "I honestly never thought about it. I saw it as a choice between having money and not."

"Think through all the possibilities, then do what you think is right. I'll support you whatever you do."

A man came up to Tad. "Your father said you'd be here. Keys to your new car. Mr. Willis didn't think you'd want to stay with the old one."

Tad took the keys. "Say thanks to my father for me. I'll drop in later and see how he's doing."

"He says the doctors will let him go home today. Suitable care has been arranged."

"Great. I'll call him."

The man nodded at Molly then left.

"You get a car delivered to you?" Molly raised her eyebrows.

"Ridiculous, isn't it, but Father is right. I don't know if I'd be able to get back in that car."

"Understandable." Molly jumped up. "Want to go have a look at the car?"

"I thought you didn't like cars." Tad took her hand as they walked out of the hospital.

"It isn't that I don't like them," Molly chose her words carefully. "But I couldn't afford one, and walking and transit work fine for now."

"I could get you a car." Tad looked at her.

"Thanks for the offer, but I don't know how to drive, so a car would be a waste." She leaned her head against his arm.

"How about driving lessons then?" Tad squeezed her hand. "It will be useful even if you don't buy a car."

"That would be fun." Molly grinned at him.

"We can stop by the testing centre and get you the book for the learner's test."

"Okay."

Tad smiled back at her. "First stop is the Drivers Test Centre."

"You know what I do need?" Molly almost stopped there. She didn't want to take advantage of Tad's money. It was his. She had to pay her own way.

"What?" Tad asked.

"My cell phone is gone. The guy took it." Molly said the words tentatively.

"Let's go look at cell phones next then." Tad opened the door for her, and she shivered. "You need a new coat too, I'm guessing.

"I do. I have money for the coat." Molly wrapped her arms around her as she followed Tad to where a bright red car was parked. He pushed the button on the key fob and its lights blinked.

Molly gratefully sat in the still warm car and felt the leather seats. She could own something like this. Did she really want it? Did she want it?"

Tad got in and started the car. "This is a heavier car, it won't be as nimble as the blue one. I bet my father had a hand in choosing it."

"It is a very nice car." Molly put on her seatbelt. She took out her wallet that had been returned the night before. The clothes she didn't want. That meant new clothes too. *My bank account is going to be empty after this.*

The car's trunk got fuller and fuller as the day passed. She insisted on buying her own coat, but Tad got her hat and gloves to go with it. The cell phone came with a zero-down plan. She winced at the monthly cost, but would have to make it work. Tad insisted on buying a protective case for it. Tad only suggested a few times that he buy something that Molly's avarice liked. She refused, but he expanded and supported her choices. They were things she would have bought for herself at some point, so she allowed it.

Tad parked and helped her carry the bags up to her apartment.

"Thank you for letting me spoil you just a bit." Tad hugged her. "I think you're the first person who has ignored the money and just looked at me. It means a lot."

"Thanks for spoiling me, just a little." Molly stood on her tiptoes and kissed him on the cheek. "I had fun today. I needed that. I'll see you Tuesday if not sooner."

Tad left with an odd look on his face. She hoped she hadn't upset him. Pulling out the paper Ferguson gave her, Molly dialled the number. Maybe she should wait for Blue to come home.

"Nancy Watson. How may I help you?"

"Sergeant Ferguson gave me your number. I'm Molly Callister."

"Ah, I was hoping you would call." Nancy said. "Tell me a little about yourself."

Molly lost track of time as she recounted her life since meeting Blue. The life before that could wait for another time, when she felt braver. Nancy was a good listener. Asking a question here or there, but mostly letting her ramble.

"O gosh, I didn't mean to talk for so long." Molly put a hand to her mouth when she saw the time.

"I got immersed in your story." Nancy laughed. "You're a good storyteller. I'll email you a package to fill out and some information on being a case study."

"Before you go, I have a question."  Molly's face grew hot and she looked around the empty apartment to be sure no one was listening. "I have been going out with this guy for a year, but I haven't been able to let him kiss me. I'm worried that time I was a sex worker will get in the way."

"Sex and love are different things." Nancy said. "Don't confuse them. Focus on the love and the rest will eventually fall into place. It has been good talking to you." She hung up and Molly heaved a sigh.

Tad had hidden himself for a year, then seemed to see her as an object. But she would get to know the other part of Tad. She didn't want to be without him right now, but time would tell.

Molly pushed the thoughts aside and got to work on supper. Blue would be home soon.

# CHAPTER 20
## Tuesday, December 2, 2022

For a change in venue, Tad took her to the Odeon in Aberdeen Mall, then to Red Robin's for coffee and a dessert.

"Where do these guys get all the guns from?" Molly sipped at her coffee. "It's ridiculous. And they never run out of ammo for any of them."

"I can't imagine trying to carry a bag with that many weapons in it. They aren't light and they put a lot in the bag." Tad took a bite of his chocolate cake.

"I did like the heroine. She was believable. A terrible shot, but good enough to cover for the hero."

"There are going to be other movies." Tad offered Molly a bite of his cake. "But having them just meet for coffee at the end was a bit of a downer."

"I think it was a smart move." Molly tried her own dessert. "They hardly knew anything about each other. It made sense to start with getting to know each other. It's great to be a good fighter, but does he cook?"

"Lots of guys cook." Tad sipped at his coffee.

"I know, but does *he* cook? The only time we see him eating at home it was cold beans out of a can."

"Okay, you are making a comment about a specific guy. But what about her? What's her skill set?"

"She's a teacher. At least she was when the movie started. Who knows what will happen after she misses a week and can't explain why."

Tad laughed and saluted her with his coffee. Molly offered him a bit of her dessert.

"What did you do this past weekend?" Tad asked. "I spent most of mine with my father."

"Ferguson and Hassim came over for dinner and we put the case to bed. Ferguson took the files with him. We had a good time. They're really nice people when you get to know them. Oh, and Ferguson dropped off my paycheck. I'd forgotten I was getting paid. It was almost two thousand dollars! I was in shock."

"Sounds like fun." Tad put his coffee down and took her hand. "I missed you."

"I missed you too." Molly smiled at him. "Ciara had her party and from what she said on Sunday it was a glorious success. She doesn't know about the case I worked on, so it was a bit surreal hearing all about her friends and the fun they had while I was still processing stopping a serial killer and almost losing my boyfriend."

"Boyfriend?" Tad turned red and had the silliest grin on his face.

"Boyfriend." Molly leaned across the table and brushed her lips over his. "I think I'm ready to hear what you want to say without panicking."

"Okay then." Tad got a mischievous look in his eyes. "I decided what to do with my money."

"Oh?" Molly told her heart not to sulk.

"Father helped me set up a foundation. I pay myself a salary and manage incoming grant applications from local agencies. We settled on a hundred thousand a year. I talked my father down a lot. But he's going to put money into the foundation. He said all the fun was earning it, so I might as well use his money too."

"A hundred thousand?" Molly couldn't imagine making that much. She barely brought in thirty thousand a year before taxes.

"He said I need to be able to maintain the condo and put gas in the car. It isn't a lot less than what I usually spend in a year."

"Right." Molly somehow got the words out. "That sounds sensible."

Tad laughed and dug into his cake. Molly attacked her cheesecake and thought hard. Three years of her salary was what Tad spent in a year. What did he do that used that much money? They finished their cake and coffee and walked out to the car.

"You okay?" Tad asked. "You're awfully quiet."

"I'm adjusting my assumptions about the world." Molly didn't look at him. "It is hard to imagine having the kind of freedom you have."

"I'm working on adjusting to more responsibility." Tad snorted. "The learning curve for running a foundation is going to be really steep. I need to start by writing out the purpose and goal, create policy and hire people to do the bookkeeping and administration."

"Will you pay them out of your hundred thousand?"

"No. I have to keep my finances at arm's length from the foundation. We'll use about ten percent of the income for running expenses. That includes renting and setting up an office."

"Sounds like a lot of work." Molly watched the lights of the city. It was a much bigger place than she knew.

"It will be good for me." Tad glanced over at her and smiled. For some reason Molly's face grew warm.

All to soon they arrived at the apartment. Tad walked her to the door.

"Should we go to the Odeon next week?"

"Why not?" Molly said. "It was fun. I'd like you to come over Friday evening and have supper with me and Blue. Give me a chance to talk about something other than movies."

Tad hugged for a long time, then whispered in her ear. "I love you."

"I think I love you too." Molly had no trouble with the words, though she'd been terrified of saying them. It just felt true. She stretched up to kiss Tad on the lips. He held her tight. She could taste the chocolate on his lips. Then he let go and stepped back.

"We could freeze to death if we kiss too long."

"It would be a good death." Molly laughed. "See you Friday."

Tad gave her one more kiss, before she slipped in the door where she watched him walk to the car, then drive away.

Touching her lips, Molly smiled, then danced up the stairs to talk to Blue.

# OTHER BOOKS BY ALEX
Series:

**Calliope Books**
Calliope and the Sea Serpent
Calliope and the Royal Engineers
The Third Prince and the Enemy's Daughter
Calliope and the Kershan Empire
Calliope and the Engine Smith

**Spruce Bay Books**
Wendigo Whispers
Cry of the White Moose
Disputed Rock

**The Belandria Tarot**
The Devil Reversed
The Regent's Reign
The Empire Unbalanced
The World Widens
The Fury Unleashed

**Blue in Kamloops**
Tranquille Dark
Columbia Smoke
Victoria Run
Rivers Trail Hun

**The Fae**
Call of a Hero
Shieldmaiden's Quest


**Stand-alone books:**

Leedles and the Golden Tree
Generation Gap
The Gods Above
Tales of Light and Dark
Like Mushrooms (poetry and photography)
The Heronmaster
Blood and Sparkles, and other stories
Princess of Boring
By the Book
Sarcasm is My Superpower
Playing on Yggdrasil
The Unenchanted Princess

Read short stories and excerpts from his novels at alexmcgilvery.com